Dear Alexandra,

I've met a woman who's knocked me for a loop. She's absolutely irresistible and really quite incredible—a baffling mixture of innocence, mystery and sublime sensuality. I can't think straight, and I can't figure her out. On the one hand, she seems as attracted to me as I am to her. On the other hand, she seems determined to shove me out of her life. And, you know, she's got this funny little quirk: when she's embarrassed, she hiccups, just like you. There's something about her. . . .

As a child, **Elise Title** was sure she'd be a writer. But when she grew up, married, had a career in social work and two children, there just wasn't any time. So she put her creative energies into planning memorable vacations and designing and renovating her home in Hanover, New Hampshire.

Her dream of writing never faded. Five years ago she finally decided to take the plunge, quit her job and devote herself full-time to writing. Her many readers are glad she did. Elise has become well established in the romance genre, with thirty novels to her credit under the name Alison Tyler.

Love Letters

ELISE TITLE

Harlequin Books

TORONTO • NEW YORK • LONDON
AMSTERDAM • PARIS • SYDNEY • HAMBURG
STOCKHOLM • ATHENS • TOKYO • MILAN

To David and Becca,
my best cheerleaders

Published May 1988

ISBN 0-373-25303-6

Prologue

San Francisco
May 5

Dear Greg,

Do you realize this is our fifth anniversary? Don't laugh. No, you wouldn't laugh. I know that. I still can't believe that we've been writing to each other for five months now. I guess you know how much it means to me.

Just think! I almost didn't take that elective in drafting. And then when I picked designing a skyscraper for my senior project and read about your fantastic award-winning skyscraper design in that architectural magazine, I never dreamed, when I got up the nerve to write you in New York for some information and help, that you'd ever write me back.

I got my paper back today. I aced it, thanks to you. And not just because of all the stuff you sent me on design schemes. You really boosted my confidence, Greg. If you hadn't kept writing me, telling me how good my project was coming along, I'd never have put so much effort into it.

You're really a special guy, Mr. Greg Hollis. Most 23-year-old men wouldn't bother to keep on writing a lowly high-school senior. Sometimes I think that maybe you keep answering my letters because you think, poor kid, she's lonely and confused and I can't let her down. I know I do go on and on about all my dumb problems with my folks and with some of the kids at school, but you always have such neat advice. And it really made me feel great when you wrote in your last letter that you think I'm mature and perceptive. And that you can understand where I'm coming from because you've been there yourself. It's hard for me to believe you've ever felt out of it or lonely or mixed up. But I guess that really is what makes our penpal friendship so special. And I don't care what you say. That dumb Beth Aarons at your firm who won't give you the time of day is a *fool!*

My graduation pictures came back yesterday. I almost sent you one. But they really came out crummy. And besides, I kind of like the idea of "maintaining the mystery." What if you didn't like the way I looked? I know what you're thinking. Friends shouldn't go by appearances. I agree. But I feel as if I know what you look like just from reading your letters. And (ha, ha) I like what I read!

Greg, wouldn't it be great if we just went on writing to each other forever? We'd never meet, never speak on the phone, never even know what each other looks like. We'd just share this incredible connection through our words. I honestly feel we have so much in common in our souls.

Okay, so now I'm blushing. And you might as well know, when I get embarrassed, my nose starts to run. When I'm real embarrassed, I start hiccuping. So since I'm out of tissues and have to run

downstairs to get one—as well as a glass...
of ... water—I'll sign off for now.

Your very close friend,
Alex

New York
June 14

Dear Alex,

I can't believe it's been nine years since we began
corresponding. We've helped each other with a lot
of problems in that time. You know, I really value
our friendship. But enough of that mushy stuff . . .

Quit the rationalizations about why you broke
it off with Sam. What does that make, Alex? Four
this year? *You're* the guidance counselor. You don't
need *me* to analyze your problem, sweetheart.
You, as the pop-pysch books are so fond of saying, have a problem with commitment. And don't
go turning the tables and telling me I have the same
problem. At least I took the risk once and tried
marriage. Let's skip where it got me. And no, I'm
not still bitter about Liz. It's been two years since
the divorce.

Okay, so maybe you're right. I guess it still
hurts—a little. Rob Holden was supposedly my
friend. Last I heard, friends aren't supposed to betray you. They certainly aren't supposed to go
running off with your wife. Then again, I was fool
enough to believe wives are supposed to be even
more faithful than friends.

You're the only one, Alex. The only one I trust.
You remain, as always, my lovely, sensitive mystery woman. There have been times over these past
nine years, I don't mind telling you, that your let-

ters were pretty much all that kept me from sinking into a state of "St. Gregory Blues" as you've so inimitably dubbed the condition. You do get on my back sometimes, but in case you haven't figured it out yet, I wouldn't want it any other way.

Things are going better with Meg. You see, I'm still willing to take a few risks. I know what you're thinking. Meg is so entrenched in her modeling career that she makes very few demands. Okay, so I'm taking the easy way out as usual. None of us is perfect. And I'm not drowning myself in my work as an excuse to avoid life. Last I noticed, my head was still above water.

Seriously, Alex, I need my work. And it feels good to have made the break into restoration architecture. You know how I feel about preserving the past. There are some things I feel are worth holding on to, some things that should never be changed. Like us.

I'm not going to say there wasn't a part of me that didn't feel sorely tempted to pick up the phone and call you when I was at that conference in San Francisco last month. Nine years and I've never so much as heard your voice. I know that no one would believe two people could write to each other all these years and not have the slightest idea what the other sounds like or looks like. When we first made that pact years ago, I thought it was a little crazy. But it really has let us both be absolutely open and honest because it's so safe this way. We both know that's what's made our relationship so special, so unique. As long as neither of us breaks the rules, we'll someday be writing each other about what it feels like to have grandchildren, to grow old....

Listen, Sam probably wasn't good enough for you, anyway. You deserve someone special. You've got so much tenderness and compassion and love in you. You just need to find the right guy and everything will click.

I know, I know. You think I sound like your mother. Only remember, Alex, your mother has never understood you. I, on the other hand, know you like a book. And to coin an old phrase I once learned from a very special teenager, I like what I read.

Love as always,
Greg

1

ALEXANDRA YATES ROLLED over to avoid the morning sunlight flooding in her window. She squinted past the letter to the alarm clock. Seven-fifteen. She studied the clock with a small frown. "I'm on vacation," she muttered to herself. "I can sleep till three in the afternoon if I want to indulge myself. And I do want to indulge myself." She stretched, her frown deepening. "What's the use? I've been conditioned. I'll probably wake up at seven-fifteen for the rest of my life."

She flung off the covers, a *Mademoiselle* magazine, a box of stationery and her cat, Menlo, and all fell with varying thuds to the floor. Menlo meowed with irritation.

"I know. You're on vacation, too." Alexandra grinned, reaching down and lifting the tiger-striped cat to her lap. As she stroked him with one hand, she flipped on the clock radio with the other. A cheery voice burst into the room announcing a brief spate of sunshine followed by another day of rain.

Alexandra's dog, Nell, made a disgruntled sound from under the bed and popped her scraggly brown head out from beneath the white dust ruffle.

Alexandra scratched the mutt's head with her toes and fell back across the bed to stare at the ceiling. "Who said vacations were for lolling around and getting fat and lazy?" She'd promised herself that once school was over, she'd exercise every morning and then take a nice healthy jog around the Presidio. She glanced toward the window. If the meteorologist was right about the rain, she'd have to get moving if she wanted to get in her jog on her first day.

Nell rested her chin on Alexandra's knee. Alexandra stretched out her hand and gave the dog another scratch. "You can come jog with me."

The mutt whimpered and retreated under the dust ruffle.

"Coward," Alexandra chided.

Menlo squirmed free and darted onto the bedside table, sending a letter from her friend Cassie fluttering onto the bed. Alexandra picked it up and scanned it again.

New York
June 14

Dear Alex,

I know it's been ages since I've written, but I'll be back in my Manhattan apartment for a few weeks on my way from Paris to Tokyo. You've simply got to fly east for a visit with your old high-school buddy. You can stay all summer if you like. My summer sublet fell through, and this apartment is a dream. After I leave, you can have it all to yourself. The new tenant doesn't move in until late August. Besides, you've got to brave the world some day. You've never even crossed the Rocky Mountains. Anyway, it's your summer vacation, so you have no excuse. Just think. We can stay up all night giggling like we did back in high school. Don't turn me down, Alex. I've been through a tough year, and I'd really love to get together with an old friend. Whoever said the fashion business

was glamorous is crazy. Sometimes I think how
nice it would be to just throw in the towel and
marry some nice guy and then only design cloth-
ing for the triplets I'd have. How about you? You
ever feel like opting for Mr. Right over women's
liberation? You can answer that question when you
arrive on my doorstep.

Love,
Cassie

Alexandra had probably read the letter a hundred
times since she'd received it the day before. And every
time she read it, she experienced the same funny tingle
in her spine.

She stared at the letter with a solemn expression. Did
she dare risk being in the same city as Greg Hollis?
What if she were tempted to phone him just as he'd been
tempted to phone her the last time he was here? She did
occasionally have a hard time resisting temptation.
And nine years of fantasizing about what Greg's voice
sounded like, never mind what he *looked* like, was a
long time.

She scowled, sitting up again. "This is ridiculous,"
she said out loud. She wouldn't call Greg. She'd probably die of embarrassment. She'd written and told him
some of her most intimate feelings. And he'd written her
about things she was certain he'd never shared with
anyone else.

She swung her long, lithe legs out of bed. "No. Greg's
absolutely right. What we share is too special to mess
with," she announced firmly, Menlo and Nell paying
little attention as they both spied a fly buzzing around
the room.

The bedroom door opened. Jill Cutler, Alexandra's roommate, popped her head into the room. "This is disgusting," the small, rounded brunette announced, waving her damp toothbrush in the air.

Alexandra grinned. "Are you referring to the state of disarray of my room, my less-than-winning morning appearance, or this embarrassing habit I have of talking to myself?"

Jill laughed. "I'm referring to the fact that if I had a two-month summer vacation instead of a dreary nine-to-fiver in an insurance office, I, for one, would not be up at seven-fifteen in the morning chatting with anyone, regardless of how many legs he or she had."

Alexandra grinned. "I'm going to jog around the Presidio." She fell back across the bed.

"I see."

"I really should start jogging. I need exercise. It's just that it's—"

"So boring?"

Alexandra sighed. "Right."

"Well, if I had a body like yours, sweetie, I wouldn't worry about exercise."

Alexandra sat up cross-legged on the bed. She knew she was lucky to have the kind of body that somehow seemed to remain limber and taut despite her lack of discipline. She still looked pretty good in a bikini, she supposed. Not as good as when she was seventeen, but for a twenty-six-year-old woman she had nothing to complain about.

"I need a change," Alexandra said, rising from the bed, stretching and then shuffling across the room. She studied her face in the mirror over her bureau, smoothing back the auburn hair that had escaped her long single braid and frizzed out softly around her face.

More than one man had told her she looked very much as if she'd stepped out of a portrait painted by one of the old masters. While meant, she supposed, as a compliment, it merely reinforced her belief that she was never to become the chic, glamorous beauty of her adolescent fantasies.

Alexandra scowled at herself in the mirror. "Maybe I'll cut my hair."

Jill merely laughed. "I've known you for six years, Miss Yates, and if you so much as *see* a beauty parlor, you cross the street for fear some maniacal hairdresser will come rushing out and start chopping that wild mane of yours."

Alexandra laughed, undoing the braid and combing through the thick strands so that her hair flew around her head. She did love her hair, even though it was hopelessly unfashionable. She loved the way it swished across her back as she moved. It gave her an exuberant feeling.

"Maybe I'll go to New York, then."

Jill eyed her closely. "Isn't that too close for comfort?"

Alexandra studied Jill in the mirror. "There are millions of people in New York. I'm not even going to tell Greg I'll be there. You could forward me his letters, and I could send my letters to him through you."

"Alex, don't you think it's ridiculous to honor this pact the two of you made nine years ago? I mean, you're not a starry-eyed teenager anymore. And Greg is...how old? Thirty-one?"

"Thirty-two."

Jill shook her head. "You're a grown woman. You've been corresponding with this guy for nine years. I think it's high time the two of you got together."

"You don't understand, Jill."

"Did you ever think he just might be the man of your dreams?"

"I'm not a starry-eyed adolescent anymore, remember? I don't have those kind of dreams."

"Who are you kidding, Alexandra Yates? None of us is ever too old to dream. I'm squeezing thirty, and let me tell you, I had a dream just last night. . . ."

"Greg is involved with someone." Alexandra pulled open a drawer and started rummaging a bit too frantically for her underwear. "Anyway, Greg knows me too well to have any romantic notions about me." She grabbed her things. "I've spilled my guts to him, Jill. And my guts are not my most attractive feature."

"Well, if Greg never gets to see your more attractive ones, how's he ever going to get romantic notions?"

Alexandra sighed with frustration. "You don't get it, Jill. I don't *want* him to have romantic notions. And *I* don't want to have any, either." She swung around to face her friend. "Greg and I share something unique, something absolutely honest. Romance would only spoil it. If we ever did meet and discovered there were . . . some sparks, all of a sudden we'd have to start worrying about saying the right thing, doing the right thing, looking good. The whole bit. No, thanks. I'm perfectly happy with the way things are between me and Greg."

Jill arched a brow. "Well, let's see what happens after you hit New York City."

New York
July 1

Dear Alex,

Guess who appeared from out of the blue last

week? My father. Typical of the man, he's conveniently forgotten our last raging encounter when I told him I was giving up my prestigious position at Elroy's to go into restoration work and he informed me that until I came to my senses he'd have nothing more to say to me.

It never ceases to amaze me that his presence alone still produces such sweeping feelings of rage and doubt inside me. He's always so damn sure of himself. The man was born without the need to doubt or question anything he does. How comforting it must be to know all the answers. And how unfortunate that his only child has proved such a disappointment to him.

Not, of course, that I gave him the slightest hint of the turmoil his arrival caused me. If nothing else, I've learned over the years to conceal my feelings well.

It turns out the old man went to see my exhibit of architectural renderings for the Gilrand Estate over at the Pierce Gallery and then showed up at my office afterward. He gave me one of those weary looks of his, a brief lecture on how I've squandered my talents and not so much as a word about the renderings. I know, I know. It's about time I stopped trying to win the man's approval. When, my perceptive Alex, will I grow up?

We went out for dinner afterward. Meg joined us. Of course, she was charmed by my father. Such a delightful, witty, self-confident man. And all that wealth and prestige to boot. She accused me later of treating him abominably, claiming I was cool, aloof and insufferably rude to the dear man. I didn't bother to argue. There's no one but you who can understand the love-hate relationship my father and I have carried on ever since my mother's death. I think you're right, Alex, that neither of us knew how to grieve. In our pain we turned against each other. But I was only a boy of fourteen at the time. He was a man. My father. When I needed him most, he let me down. His solution to my grief was to send me off to a military boarding school so that I could build some backbone. Well, I built some, all right.

But that's in the past. I'm older and wiser now, right? Besides, he left the next morning before we could get into one of our typical go-arounds. His last words to me were that I was a difficult man. I swear, Alex, I had to laugh. Of course, he then accused me of feeling superior to him.

In a way, I suppose he was the one who ended up getting the last laugh. The next day Meg phoned and told me we were through. It seems she, too, has decided I'm a difficult man. There must be some conspiracy afoot. Than again, maybe they're both right. What do you think?

Love as always,
"St. Gregory"

Alexandra set the letter down and closed her eyes. She wanted to cry. No, that wasn't the feeling exactly. She really wanted to reach out and put her arms around Greg. She knew how much he was hurting. If he was "difficult," there were plenty of extenuating circumstances. She probably knew that better than anyone. His latest letter produced such an intense feeling that she began to tremble.

Cassie Phillips looked up from a design she was working on at her drafting table at the other end of the living room. "Are you all right, Alex?"

Alexandra's heart was pounding and her stomach churned. "I shouldn't have come to New York."

Cassie frowned. "An upsetting letter from your eternal penpal?"

Alexandra's eyes narrowed.

Cassie raised a hand. "Okay, I'm sorry. That was uncalled-for. But really, Alex, I can't believe you haven't even told the man that you're here in New York. Isn't that breaking the rules? You always said that you and Greg had a no-holds-barred, honest relationship."

"I couldn't tell him," Alexandra said in a weak voice. "And don't think it doesn't eat away at me. I should have followed my instincts and stayed put in San Francisco."

"Boloney." Cassie was never one to mince words. "If you really trusted your instincts, you'd pick up the phone right now, call the man and tell him to meet you for a drink. It would serve you right if he turned out to be short, fat and bald. Only I happen to have seen a photo of him in *New York Magazine* a year back when they were covering some skyscraper he'd designed. The man is definitely not hard on the eyes."

"Stop it, Cassie. I don't want to know what Greg looks like. I don't want to phone him. I don't want to have a drink with him. I want everything to go on exactly as it has."

"Nine years." Cassie sighed. "It's really incredible. I can't imagine what it is the two of you have found to write each other about all these years. But whether you want my opinion or not, Alex, I honestly don't think it's healthy. Or realistic. You're too wrapped up in this thing. I think Greg is the real reason you've never let yourself get serious about a man."

While her tone was scolding, Cassie's eyes showed such affectionate concern that Alexandra felt her own eyes blur with tears.

Cassie left her drawing board to go over to her friend. She put a comforting arm around her.

"Maybe you ought to just see him and get it over with."

Alexandra shook her head.

"Don't you see that you've allowed yourself to idealize the man? No one else could ever measure up. In the end, some guy will come along and win by default. That's not going to be fair to either one of you."

"You don't understand," Alexandra said, her tears giving way to exasperation. "No one understands... but me and Greg."

Cassie watched Alexandra cross the room to the front door. "I'm not sure you two understand what's really going on, either," she said softly.

Alexandra opened the door, then glanced over her shoulder at her friend. "Maybe you're right," she said slowly, a faint smile on her lips. "Give me a few more years and maybe we'll sort it out."

A couple of minutes later Alexandra stepped out of the lobby of the apartment building on Fifth Avenue into a gray drizzle. She thought of going back upstairs for a raincoat, but it wasn't raining hard and she thought, optimistically, that it would stop soon, so she merely turned left and began walking briskly down the street. She had no destination in mind. She just needed to get out, to think. As was so often the case, she found herself composing her next letter to Greg in her mind. She once again considered telling him that she had come to New York, but even though the deceit weighed heavily on her, she knew she'd say nothing about it. It was her only protection. Despite her cries to the contrary, she'd been tempted to call him a hundred times since she'd arrived in town.

Even though Greg had written her about his temptation to call her the last time he was in San Francisco, Alexandra believed that Greg felt far fewer conflicts about the rules of their relationship than she did. She sensed that the built-in anonymity was very liberating for him. In a way, it was true for her, as well. But while she tried very hard to deny it, there was a part of her that longed to make a further connection to Greg. His most recent letter, coupled with this new physical proximity, was stimulating more temptation than she'd bargained for.

The rain began in earnest when she was about four blocks from Cassie's place. Wet splotches dotted her light blue cotton dress, and her hair, pulled back with a tortoiseshell barrette, began to frizz around her face. As a few people, all suitably attired in raincoats, glanced at her in passing, Alexandra felt foolish, frumpy and very damp.

Looking for shelter from the downpour, she turned the corner and came upon a stretch of shops on East Fifty-seventh Street. She held her breath as she spotted the name Pierce Gallery toward the end of the block. Goose bumps broke out along her arms. The Pierce Gallery was where Greg's architectural drawings were being shown.

Was it only pure chance that had led her to this spot? Or was it fate? All Alexandra knew was that it hadn't been some unconscious plan of hers. Greg had never mentioned a word about the location of the gallery.

There were a half-dozen other shops she could have chosen for shelter, but she gave the other options no more than a moment's thought.

She felt an almost illicit thrill as she opened the heavy glass door to the gallery. She paused just inside, feeling a need to compose herself. As the door closed behind her, a small bell jingled. Absently she brushed back some curled tendrils from her cheek only to have them spring back rebelliously.

A smart-looking blonde sat behind the decorative teak reception desk talking on the phone. She paused for a moment in her muted conversation to give Alexandra a brief glance.

"Would you please sign our visitors' book?"

Alexandra stared at the open leather-bound book on the desk. Her first instinct was to turn and run, but with more than a little effort she pulled herself together. She approached the desk, hesitated for a moment with pen poised and then scrawled the name Cassie Phillips.

The receptionist had returned to her phone conversation, but when she noticed that Alexandra had omitted an address, she gave a small, impatient nod.

Alexandra pretended not to notice; she felt guilty enough writing Cassie's name. But she couldn't very well sign her own. What if Greg were to skim through the book sometime? Fortunately she hadn't written him about Cassie for years, and before then only in passing. She was certain the name wouldn't ring a bell for Greg.

Turning away from the scene of her deceit, Alexandra looked around the main hall of the gallery, noting several other people milling about the large, well-lit space, studying with varying degrees of interest the collection of post-Impressionist drawings that hung on the stark white walls. At first Alexandra thought that Greg's exhibition must have ended. But as she stepped farther into the gallery, she saw an archway off to the right, which led to a separate small exhibit room. Even from this distance she could see the dome-covered table in the center of the room where an elaborate model of what was very likely the Gilrand Estate was on display.

Taking a steadying breath, Alexandra crossed the room and stepped through the archway. Once inside the display room she stood absolutely still. Her focus was narrowed to this one single space, this one moment in time, this stunning sense of communion she suddenly experienced. Greg's work filled the room, but it was not his drawings nor the exquisite detailed cardboard model that she was reacting to—it was Greg's presence itself.

After a few moments she began walking slowly around the room, moving from one architectural rendering to the next. Tears filled her eyes as she studied each one. Greg's touch, so elegant and fine, was in every line, every stroke.

Alexandra crossed her arms, hugging herself in an effort to stem her trembling. She felt truly frightened by the stinging intensity of her emotions. An inner voice told her to bolt, and yet she felt compelled to stay, compelled to stare fiercely at the work of a man she knew in some ways better than she knew herself.

She was so lost in her own feelings that it took her several minutes to realize she wasn't alone.

A small gasp of surprise escaped her lips as she saw a tall, dark-haired man observing her, his hazel eyes glinting with a seductive amusement she found disturbing and irritating. The last thing in the world Alexandra wanted right now was to fend off an advance from some flirtatious stranger.

"Don't tell me you find these drawings all that enthralling." The man's thick brows lifted a fraction.

The way her chocolate-brown eyes took on an abruptly cool, hostile look made his mouth curl upward. "I see," he went on, ignoring her lack of response. "A true lover of architecture, then."

"A true believer in people minding their own business," Alexandra said sharply.

"Personally I find this kind of thing rather dry," he went on blithely.

Alexandra was pretty sure she was being baited. She was also pretty sure this was not a man who was easily thwarted. Nor, she was distressed to admit, was he easy to ignore. For one thing, he was damn attractive, his strong-boned face with its sharp angles and planes roughly sensuous. And his belted trench coat only served to highlight his lean, muscular frame. For another thing, he seemed intent on engaging her in conversation.

She walked on to the next drawing a few feet away and forced herself to concentrate on a sketch of what the facade of the Gilrand Estate would look like in its restored state.

"Do you know the mansion?" the stranger asked, moving along beside her.

She shook her head.

"It's only a few blocks from here. Since you find these drawings so fascinating, you ought to take a look at the real thing. It's actually quite a remarkable example of a nineteenth-century Gothic design—very lacy. To some, overbearingly frilly, even silly. Actually, it's a miracle it wasn't torn down for some bland skyscraper.

Now, with the recent press it's been given, if the estate is restored faithfully to the original design, it will become quite a landmark."

"If these drawings are any indication, I'm sure the restoration will be perfect. It's obvious the architect has taken painstaking care in his research and technique," Alexandra said solemnly.

He found himself smiling again as he took in the defiant lift of her chin. "The architect is very flattered," he said in a low, seductive voice.

For an instant his words didn't fully penetrate. When they did, they exploded inside Alexandra's head like a bombshell.

2

"I'VE HAD WOMEN FALL for me before, but never quite so dramatically."

Alexandra stared dazedly up into a handsome stranger's smiling face. "What . . . ?"

"Take it easy," he said soothingly as she tried to lift her head. "Just lie still for a few more minutes."

A wave of dizziness made her decide to follow his advice. As she let her head fall back, she realized for the first time that she was lying on a leather couch in an unfamiliar room. She also realized, with sick recall, who the man was staring down at her with a mixture of amusement and concern.

She let her eyes close. *No*, she thought, *this can't be happening. I've got to get out of here. I've spoiled everything.*

It was only when Greg's fingers brushed away an errant tear running down her cheek that she realized she was crying.

"Hey, it can't be all that bad," he said gently.

His tenderness only made her feel worse. She tried to keep her eyes shut, but she felt compelled to open them.

Nine years. Nine years of fantasy. Did he look the same as she'd imagined? Alexandra stared up into his half-laughing, watchful eyes. Hazel eyes. Warm hazel eyes. Yes, the eyes fit her fantasy. Greg Hollis would have eyes like this. Tender, loving eyes. And strong, rugged features. She studied his broad, angular face: the firm, square jaw, the tiny lines crinkling the corners of his sensuous mouth and compelling eyes, the thick, dark brows that matched dark brown hair worn in a careless, somewhat long fashion that, Alexandra was dismayed to discover, looked even better than in her fantasies.

She was so intent on her study it took her a moment to realize that Greg was smiling broadly.

"What do you think? Worth falling into a dead faint for?"

Alexandra decided it was the cockiest, absolutely the most infuriating grin she'd ever seen. Not to mention the sexiest, and most devastating.

She sat up abruptly, ignoring the blur of everything in the room—everything but Greg Hollis, that is.

"Where am I?" she demanded hoarsely, struggling to clear her head.

"In Richard Pierce's private office."

"Oh?" She looked around, her vision clearing as the dizziness abated.

"Richard is an old friend of mine. It was his idea to show my drawings for the Gilrand Estate here at his gallery. In fact, Richard's the one who started the ball rolling on getting the city to agree to the preservation of the mansion."

Alexandra wasn't really paying attention. "I have to go." She stood, her legs more than a little wobbly.

Greg's large hand circled her wrist. "I'll lay odds you haven't had any lunch today. What you need right now is a good meal. After that we can talk about what's troubling you. Sometimes talking to a stranger helps. Just think. I can be perfectly objective since I don't know a thing about you."

Alexandra felt positively ill. If she didn't get out of there fast, she was afraid she might pass out again. "No . . . really." Just his touch made her tremble in earnest again.

Greg was quick to point that out to her, proof that a hearty meal was just what the doctor would order. He wasn't nearly as quick to release her. "I have to insist. After all, I feel responsible."

She met his provocative gaze and felt her cheeks grow warm. "Don't be ridiculous." The words came out shakily, severely blunting their impact.

"I've got a great idea," he said, swinging his arm around her now in a paternal fashion and guiding her toward the office door. "We'll pick up some deli food and go have a picnic."

"A picnic?" The suggestion was so ludicrous that Alexandra momentarily forgot her panic. She came to an abrupt halt and glanced out the window. "It's still pouring outside."

He leaned his head toward her conspiratorially. "Haven't you ever had an indoor picnic?"

She gave him a wary glance.

"My intentions are, as they say, honorable. I don't usually pick up women this way, I swear."

Despite her continued agitation, Alexandra could feel herself slipping. A faint smile curved her lips. "I don't usually fall into a dead faint."

His hazel eyes sparkled. "Good."

Their eyes met and held for a long instant. It was Alexandra who turned away first, feeling an ache begin to grow deep inside her.

Greg's eyes continued to linger. As he studied her, he unbelted his trench coat. "You'd better put this on."

"No, no, I couldn't."

"I admit it's not exactly chic, but it will keep you dry."

"No. You don't understand. I can't. I mean I can't go to lunch with you."

"Why?"

"I . . . I don't even know you. I don't do this . . . kind of thing."

He grinned. "We've already covered that ground." He continued undoing his trench coat and slipped it off.

When he held it out for her, she backed away.

"Don't argue, Cassie. You don't want me to feel guilty for causing you pneumonia as well as a dizzy spell."

Alexandra's mouth dropped. He'd called her Cassie. Of course. The visitors' book. He must have checked it to find out who she was while she was out cold.

She felt breathless, panicky. Things were getting more complicated by the minute. Not only had she broken their cardinal rule—silently she argued that it wasn't really her fault, for how was she to know Greg would choose this particular day and time to arrive at the gallery?—but she was now trapped into an insane impersonation to boot.

What do I do now? she thought as her breath came more unevenly and a cold chill traveled down her spine. She bit down on her lower lip. There was only one thing to do.

"I've got to leave," she said, her voice raised in agitation. But even as she spoke, an inexplicable longing warred with her common sense.

He took hold of her shoulders, looking down at her with those deep, warm, hazel eyes. "I'm really a very respectable man, Miss Phillips. If you're nervous, I can even give you references." He was smiling warmly. "Come on. I was going to surprise you, but my plan was to grab some food and take you over to the Gilrand Estate. You seemed really interested in my renderings. Wouldn't you like to see the real thing? I can give you a great tour. The building itself is magnificent. Of course it's badly run-down, but no amount of rack and ruin can keep the beauty from shining through."

She opened her mouth to protest, but no sound came out. Somewhere on the way from her brain to her mouth the words had taken a detour. Alexandra felt helpless, all of her thoughts frozen, as she stared up into Greg Hollis's beguiling face.

He smiled, taking her silence for acquiescence. When he opened the door, Alexandra's feet moved forward one in front of the other, seemingly of their own accord.

Okay, so she'd have lunch with him, she decided as she allowed him to throw his trench coat over her shoulders and steer her out of the gallery. After all, the damage was already done, as it were. One lunch. She'd allot herself an hour. One brief hour, no more, and she'd vanish into the city, never to see him again. How could she fight the temptation now that she'd actually discovered Greg Hollis was more alluring than she'd fantasized?

She stuck her hands into the overlong sleeves of Greg's coat as they dashed across Fifty-seventh Street. He took hold of her hand, his grasp firm. When they made it safely through the traffic to the other side of the street, their eyes met. They both grinned.

And then, perhaps because Alexandra knew she looked so outlandishly silly in Greg's oversize coat and because Greg looked so irresistible with the rain steaming down his face, she broke into laughter.

"You're a funny sort," Greg said.

"Definitely not one of your typical New York glamour girls."

"Thank goodness." He grinned.

They dashed into an empty corner delicatessen. While she left the ordering to Greg, Alexandra leaned against the storefront window, a faint smile on her lips. Now that she had consigned herself to the careless whim of fate, she made up her mind that she might as well stop worrying. She even managed to think, briefly, that everything would work out just fine.

"Pickles, right?" Greg called to her.

"How'd you guess?"

"A flash of intuition," he said, winking.

A little alarm went off inside her head. Too many flashes and there was likely to be a heart-wrenching explosion. Her brief moment of mindless abandon deserted her to be replaced by a wave of guilt. And fear.

A difficult man, indeed. He was anything but. If only Greg had been cool and arrogant and as impossible as his father and Meg had accused him of being.

Meg. Of course, Alexandra thought with a sinking sensation in the pit of her stomach. Not even two weeks had gone by since Meg had called Greg and broken off their relationship. Greg was very likely nursing a severely bruised ego. Perhaps he was looking for someone to help him nurse his wounds.

"I've got everything except the wine," Greg said, walking over to her. "There's a store that sells liquor near the house. Ready?" He shifted the deli bag to one arm, using his free hand to reach out and lift up the collar of the trench coat. His fingers lightly brushed her neck.

At his touch Alexandra let out an involuntary little shudder.

He studied her closely. "You still look a little pale. Are you okay?"

Alexandra's eyes widened. *Okay? No, I'm not okay. I'm as far from okay as a person can be.* Aloud she said weakly, "I'm fine."

"I think we ought to hop a cab over to the mansion. Why don't you wait here and I'll see if I can find us one?" He grinned. "It's usually murder to get a taxi in this weather, but I feel lucky today."

Alexandra managed a faint smile.

He set the bag on a nearby table and started for the door.

"Wait," she called out, quickly unbuttoning the coat. "Take this."

He nodded, slipping it on.

Alexandra's smile broadened. "It looks better on you."

Greg shook his head. "I don't know about that." He stood at the doorway but didn't step outside immediately. Instead, he turned back to her, giving her a slow, considering look.

"You're not from New York, are you?"

A shiver crept down her back. "No." The word was a bare whisper.

"Just visiting?"

Alexandra swallowed hard, managing another faint no. Finding her voice, she said more strongly, "I've been here for a while, but . . . my work takes me . . . away a lot."

He cocked his head at a very appealing angle. "What kind of work is that?"

She could feel herself sinking deeper and deeper into her self-dug hole. "I . . . work . . . for a fashion designer. As her . . . assistant."

He smiled. It was such an innocent smile that Alexandra wanted to cry. In nine years she could not think of one fib she'd ever told Greg. And now in the space of little more than nine minutes she'd told him nothing but lies.

He was still studying her face. Alexandra had the sickening feeling he could somehow see right through her. She didn't even have the sense to give him a casual smile and shove him out the door in search of the cab. She just stood there, feeling guilty, awkward, embarrassed. There was a part of her that longed to bridge the distance between them, to tell him the truth, to reach out and touch him, but. . . .

She could feel her nose start to run. Abruptly she turned around and grabbed a napkin from a metal holder on one of the empty Formica tables lining one wall of the delicatessen and blew her nose.

She turned back to Greg with a shaky smile. "I guess I am coming down with a cold." Her voice cracked a bit. "My throat is sore."

It was Greg who bridged the distance between them, his hand pressing gently to her forehead. "You do feel warm."

"I . . . think I'd better . . . head home."

"I'll tell you what. We'll postpone the tour of the Gilrand Estate for another day and have our picnic back at your place instead."

"No," she said, so sharply that he gave her a queer look.

"Don't tell me you've got someone back there. Husband? Boyfriend?"

"No . . . no," she muttered inanely.

"You are a strange one, Cassie Phillips." His smile was mischievous. "That's definitely part of your appeal." He gave her an affectionate tap under her chin with his index finger. "You are very appealing, you know. Or maybe you don't know." He squeezed her arm lightly and winked. "Don't go away. I'll be back in a minute." His voice was low, with a note of intimate reassurance.

Alexandra remained mute, feeling something deep inside her turn over at the fierce pull of his attraction.

He opened the door and was gone, disappearing into the storm.

Alexandra caught the eye of the heavyset clerk behind the deli counter. He gave her a broad wink. She gave him a sickly smile, then glanced around the empty restaurant. The walls seemed to whirl and revolve around her, and she suddenly felt a lot like Alice in Wonderland whose temptations had led her straight down that rabbit's hole and on to one mind-boggling adventure after another.

Casting a quick glance out the storefront window at Greg, who was standing on the corner searching the rain-soaked streets for an empty cab, Alexandra hurried over to the deli counter, her resolve firm.

"Is there a back entrance to this place?"

The clerk gave her a funny look.

"Please," she entreated.

The man shrugged. "Past the sign for the rest rooms."

She gave him a grateful smile.

"You're gonna miss out on a fantastic meal. Especially those pickles," he called out to her as she raced toward the back.

Alexandra didn't doubt it.

Ten minutes later, drenched to the bone and looking very much like something even the cat wouldn't drag in, Alexandra leaned against the door to Cassie's apartment. She closed her eyes momentarily, catching her trembling lips between her teeth and fighting to stem the maelstrom of her emotions.

Her eyes were raw, her throat was raw, her whole body felt raw. With one hand steadying her other, she managed to get the key Cassie had given her into the lock.

Cassie was still working at her drawing board when the door opened. One look at Alexandra and she let out a sharp cry.

"My God, Alex. What happened to you?" She hurried over as Alexandra shut the door and fell weakly against it.

"I . . . I'm fine. I just . . . got caught in the . . . storm."

"Caught in it. You look like it beat you to a pulp." Cassie took her firmly by the hand and led her toward the spare bedroom. "You better get those wet things off instantly and climb into a hot bath. While you're soaking, I'll whip up a nice, stiff hot toddy for you."

Just as Alexandra was about to slip inside her room, Cassie took hold of her shoulder. "You're sure nothing...terrible...happened to you? No one tried to mug you or anything like that?"

A small sigh escaped Alexandra's lips. "Nothing like that," she said in little more than a whisper.

Cassie frowned. "Something is wrong. You look . . . upset. I wish you'd tell me about it, Alex." Her frown deepened. Then she sighed. "But I suppose you always have your loving penpal, Greg Hollis, to share your troubles with. No need to ever share them with anyone else."

Tears spilled out of Alexandra's eyes, and Cassie, while baffled by her friend's reaction, was instantly contrite.

"I'm sorry, Alex. Maybe I'm just jealous. It must be nice to have a man out there to bare your soul to. Look, you get undressed and I'll start filling the tub for you. I've got some terrific French bubble bath that I'll throw in free of charge," Cassie said with a grin.

Alexandra didn't have the energy to even muster a small smile. She merely nodded and shuffled into her room. After she pried the wet clothes from her damp body, she sat down on the edge of the bed and let her head drop into her palms.

Lies upon lies. Somehow she couldn't bring herself to tell Cassie about her fateful encounter. She wasn't sure why. Perhaps she simply wanted to pretend it had never happened.

But it *had* happened. Greg was no longer a fantasy composed of nothing more than a huge drawerful of letters. He was a living, breathing man. A man that far surpassed her juvenile dreams. And his being attracted to her made her feel doubly distraught, doubly confused. There'd been an electric current between them. She'd more than felt it. The current had threatened to consume her.

"Your bath's ready."

Cassie's voice broke through her disturbing thoughts. "Thanks, Cass. I'll be . . . right out."

Alexandra slipped on her terry robe and crossed the room. When she opened the door, Cassie scrutinized her carefully. "You look like you might be running a fever. Maybe I should call a doctor."

Alexandra managed a smile. "Don't be silly. I'm probably coming down with a cold. I'll be fine by tomorrow."

"Well, I think I'll cancel my dinner date for tonight and just make sure you—"

Alexandra cut her off. "No, I don't need looking after, honest. I'll make myself a bowl of soup and climb into bed early. You go have a good time."

"Are you sure?"

"I'm positive."

Cassie hesitated. "I can at least skip my hair appointment this afternoon if you want some company."

Alexandra smiled, touched by Cassie's concern. She grabbed a handful of her friend's shoulder-length blond hair and tugged it gently. "Go to the beauty parlor. You don't want your hair to start looking like mine, do you?" she teased. Then she undid the tortoiseshell barrette at the nape of her neck, and her wild auburn hair sprung out in thick, rambunctious waves.

Cassie stared at Alexandra and shook her head slowly. "You don't know, do you?"

Alexandra's eyes narrowed. "Know what?"

Cassie smiled affectionately and gave a small shrug. "Oh . . . how special you look."

Alexandra flushed. "Don't be ridiculous, Cass. When I see some of those chic women walking in and out of those high-priced Fifth Avenue department stores with their designer clothes, designer purses, even their designer shopping bags, I feel like a complete frump. I don't know, Cass. Maybe New York just isn't my kind of town. Actually—" she hesitated "—I've been thinking I might head back home early."

Cassie's eyes narrowed. "Alex, there's nothing in San Francisco to hurry back to."

Alexandra opened the bathroom door and stepped inside. "I know," she said, closing the door behind her.

Cassie remained on the other side. "You need to start making some changes in your life, Alex. You're really in a rut."

Alexandra took off her robe and stepped into the soothingly warm bubble bath. "I know."

"So stay in the city for the summer. Experience something different. Go shopping on Fifth Avenue. Buy yourself a chic new wardrobe. Let me fix you up with a couple of classy guys. Let yourself go a little, Alex. What do you say?"

Alexandra leaned her head against the inflated bath pillow at the end of the tub. "I don't know," she said with a sigh as tears slipped down her cheeks.

Cassie opened the bathroom door a crack. "Hey—" she smiled sympathetically "—tears are murder on the bubbles. And that stuff cost a fortune. Enjoy it a little."

Alexandra sniffed. "I really have become an old stick-in-the-mud." She wrinkled her brow. "On the other hand, maybe I've never grown up. I feel so confused, Cassie. That's probably why I do so well as a high-school guidance counselor. I can really relate to those kids. When they sit in my office looking at me with those fresh yet bewildered faces and tell me they don't know what they want to do with their lives, let me tell you, Cass, I can truly empathize with them."

"So," Cassie asked, leaning against the doorjamb, "what do you want, kid?"

Alexandra shrugged. "I wish I knew. Maybe...a different career. Something with more excitement, travel. A chance to meet lots of new people, feel challenged."

Cassie shook her head. "It isn't all it's cracked up to be, Alex. Not when, at the end of each day, you walk into an empty room and there's no one to share your excitement...or your troubles. And I'm not speaking out of jealousy when I say that writing to some guy, however intimately, just isn't the same thing as putting

your arms around a man you love and feeling his loving arms wrapped around you. Get my drift?"

Alexandra slowly lifted her eyes in Cassie's direction. "I get it."

"You really are hung up on him, aren't you? And if
you ask me who, I'm going to drown you in those bubbles, Miss Yates."

Wavering between "I'm not sure" and "More than
you'll ever know," Alexandra ruminated over her
choices. The doorbell rang, and Cassie went off to see
who it was.

When Cassie opened the door, her mouth dropped
open. She'd only seen a photo of Greg Hollis once, a
long time ago. It was only this morning that she'd
mentioned it to Alexandra. But there were some men
who had unforgettable faces. Greg Hollis was one of
them.

His eyes, looking more steely gray now than hazel,
narrowed as he met the attractive blonde's stunned
gaze. For a fleeting moment he wondered if she, too,
were on the verge of passing out. What in the world was
happening?

"Cassie Phillips," he said coolly.

Cassie could only nod.

"Well," Greg said impatiently, "is she here or isn't
she?"

Cassie's expression grew even more bewildered.
"What?"

"This is the home of Cassie Phillips, isn't it?" He
threaded his fingers through his wet hair, a deep frown
on his face.

Cassie nodded. "How'd you get up here without
buzzing downstairs?"

"I walked in with one of your neighbors. I guess I have an honest face." He pressed his hand against the door. "Look, I just want to talk to her for a moment. I don't appreciate her disappearing act." His tone was sharp, irritated.

"Her disappearing act?"

Greg gave Cassie a closer look. "Are you the designer?"

"Uh...yes."

"And are you Cassie's friend as well as her employer?"

She merely stared wide-eyed at Greg, finding no answer whatsoever to that question. Instead, she asked one of her own. "You know...Cassie Phillips?"

"I don't pretend to know her at all. Actually, she's the most baffling woman I've ever run across." His eyes narrowed. "She didn't tell you about our...encounter today, then?"

Cassie slowly shook her head, but a small light was beginning to flicker on. She cast a quick glance back at the closed bathroom door and then returned her gaze to Greg. "So...you met Cassie today for the first time?"

"At a gallery. She was looking at my renderings for a restoration job I'm beginning. She seemed to have a real interest in architecture."

"Oh," Cassie said, a smile spreading across her face, "she does. She loves architecture. Especially restoration work. You might say she has a secret passion for it."

It was Greg's turn to wear a slightly bewildered expression at this woman's abrupt change in manner. "Would you please tell Cassie I'd like to talk to her for a minute?"

Cassie was positively beaming now. She took hold of the sleeve of Greg's wet trench coat and drew him into the apartment. "Come on in. Cassie's in the tub. The poor thing looked positively dreadful when she came in. But then, she's got her troubles," Cassie commented with a sigh. "I was just about to make her a hot toddy, but I'm running late for a hair appointment. How about you making one for her? And one for yourself, while you're at it. You look like you could use something soothing right about now."

Greg grinned. "Sounds like a great idea."

Cassie pulled her rain poncho off the hall tree and threw it over her head.

"Don't you think you ought to let Cassie know I'm here?"

She arched a brow. "No," she said firmly. "Why don't we just continue to leave everything to the hands of fate."

As she opened the front door to leave, Cassie chuckled. Greg watched her exit, shaking his head with a bemused smile. Then he removed his wet coat, hung it on a hook and started across the living room.

He was halfway to the kitchen on the other side of the room when the bathroom door opened.

Greg turned slowly to face the stunned, auburn-haired beauty wrapped in the white terry robe. He grinned.

"Just give me a nod of warning if you're planning to pass out on me again," he said.

3

THE SILENCE BETWEEN THEM seemed to stretch on and on. Alexandra wasn't going to faint again, though. The tension coursing through her body held her too rigid for collapse.

Greg's grin had vanished, to be replaced by a look that was somewhere between bafflement and outraged pride.

Alexandra clutched the tie of the terry robe with both hands to stem their trembling. "How did you get in here?" Her eyes darted anxiously around the room. "Where's...?" She was about to ask where Cassie was. Not knowing how to finish the sentence, she let it hang.

"Your boss?" Greg finished for it for her.

She felt a nervous twinge in her stomach.

"She had to run to the beauty parlor." Greg circled Alexandra and crossed the room. "She left me in charge. I'm supposed to make us both a hot toddy." He turned to face her and gave her a close look. "But I think you'd better eat something first. You still look a little shaky to me."

The man had a way with understatements. "Get out...please." She could feel her cheeks burning as she spoke. Another minute and she was going to start hiccuping wildly. That was one habit she'd never broken.

His gaze became a long, hard, calculating study. "Well, at least you haven't forgotten your manners."

"Look, I'm sorry about dashing off the way I did," she said defensively. "I should have said something to you, but I—"

He held up his hand. "Don't." Then, without another word, he abruptly turned and headed toward the front door.

Alexandra told herself she should feel relieved. *Don't say another word*, she cautioned silently. *Let him go and you'll be home free.*

But it wouldn't be that simple and Alexandra knew it. Nothing concerning her relationship with Greg Hollis would ever be simple again.

He was opening the door, about to make his exit.

"Wait." Her voice was little more than a strangled whisper.

He paused, glanced over his shoulder at her, smiled faintly and then continued out the door.

As she watched him go, misery swept through her. She shut her eyes for a moment and tried telling herself it was for the best.

But the thought was little consolation.

When she opened her eyes, she saw that Greg had left the front door ajar. Sighing wearily, she crossed the room to close it.

A hand shot out as she started to shut the door. Releasing her grasp on the doorknob, she silently watched the door open wider until she was once again face-to-face with Greg, who was now holding the bag of food from the deli.

"I left this stuff out in the hall. I wanted to make sure you were here before I brought it inside."

Alexandra could smell the pungent scent of pickles sneaking through their waxed-paper wrapping.

He glanced from the bag of delicacies to Alexandra. "What do you say?" He stepped inside the door, not waiting for her reply.

Alexandra didn't know what to say. The shock of not one but two encounters with Greg Hollis left her feeling deranged. Her one hope was that it was only temporary.

Greg moved closer to her.

An involuntary shiver coursed through Alexandra's body.

He shook his head in puzzlement. "What is it about me, Miss Phillips, that makes you so jittery?"

She didn't respond. She couldn't.

He took another step inside and shut the door behind him.

Alexandra backed up, bumping into a hall table. She clutched the edge for stability.

Greg cocked his head and smiled wryly. "The second question is, what is it about you, Miss Phillips, that's got my head spinning?"

"Don't call me Miss Phillips," she whispered, her breath shallow.

"Okay," he agreed good-humoredly. "How about this? What is going on with the two of us, Cassie?" He smiled playfully, but for Alexandra the whole situation was pure drama. The kind that you know from the start is going to have an unhappy ending.

"I swear," he went on conversationally, "I can't figure it out." He set the bag of deli food on the coffee table in the living room and folded his arms across his chest, his eyes scanning her face. "I can't figure out why you took off like you did and, to tell you the truth, I can't figure out exactly why I tracked you down." He reached out and touched her lightly on the cheek. "I think a part of it, anyway, is that you seem to be a woman who needs looking after." He paused, a slow smile curving his lips. "That's just part of it, though."

His seductive words and tender caress gave Alexandra a disturbingly sensual thrill. The rush of desire sent her into an even deeper panic, but her mind as well as her body seemed immobilized.

Greg picked up the bag. "Damn. I think the pickles are beginning to leak through. Where's the kitchen?"

Her body seemed to be on automatic pilot. Her hand lifted and a finger pointed of its own accord in the right direction.

"I hate skipping lunch myself," he said, disappearing into the kitchen. "Makes me feel kind of light-headed." His head popped out for a moment. "Know what I mean?"

Alexandra gave a wan smile, and he disappeared again. She could hear him in the kitchen rummaging through drawers and cupboards.

"Where do you keep your can opener?"

Alexandra didn't have the foggiest idea where Cassie kept the can opener. She sighed heavily. *I don't have the energy to keep this up*, she thought with mounting despair. *I just don't.*

"Never mind. I found it."

Alexandra smiled ruefully. Saved by the bell. How many more bells could she count on? She sank onto the bright chintz living-room couch, the colorful print making her feel queasy. Her head was pounding in earnest now, and she had no idea how she was going to make it through the rest of the day.

"You're really not okay, are you?"

Caught up in her own thoughts, Alexandra was startled by Greg's voice. Her eyes darted to the kitchen entry where he was standing, watching her intently. She shook her head slowly.

He walked over to the couch and sat down beside her. He cupped her chin and tilted her head up, placing his free hand on her forehead. "You do still feel a little warm."

His hand felt large and smooth on her skin.

He slid his hands to her shoulders and stood, taking her with him. Alexandra was too weak to offer any resistance.

"You'd better crawl into bed," he said firmly.

His shoulders were broad. He stood a good six inches taller than her. Alexandra liked big men.

"Lead the way."

Alexandra couldn't muster a protest. She took a couple of steps away from the chintz-covered couch only to feel herself losing her balance. Greg grabbed her before she lost it completely.

"Oh my goodness," she muttered in astonishment.

"What is it?"

"I really must be sick."

A wry smile pulled at the corners of his mouth. "It's beginning to look that way."

They stared at each other for a long, motionless moment. Then without a word he lifted her in his arms.

Alexandra shivered, her pulse erratic as Greg nestled her against his broad, hard chest. She looked into his face, but his features were suddenly indistinct. His grip tightened, pressing her more firmly to the muscled contours of his body.

"You really should go," she muttered, her gaze fixed hypnotically on the blurred line of his mouth. "I could be . . . contagious."

He laughed softly. "I haven't a doubt in the world about that, princess."

Alexandra's head fell heavily against his shoulder. Princess. That sounded nice. Better than Cassie, anyway.

Since she gave him no directions, Greg ended up carrying her into Cassie's bedroom. She almost said something, but then bit down on her lower lip. As he gently lowered her to the bed, Alexandra's mind flooded with new worries. What had Cassie made of Greg's arrival? What had he said to her? What had she said to Greg? What was going to happen when Cassie returned?

Alexandra sighed. It was all too much to sort out. Especially with her head spinning the way it was. Well, at least Cassie hadn't given her away. That was something.

She looked up at Greg and saw his eyes flick down over her terry robe, which had fallen open just enough to be provocative. Before she could do anything about her state of undress, Greg grabbed the spare blanket at the bottom of the bed and tossed it up over her.

She smiled gratefully.

Greg frowned. His fingers raked absently through his hair, still damp from the rain. "You'd better get some sleep...." he muttered hoarsely.

"I'm sorry, Greg. I know I'm behaving weirdly."

"Nothing to be sorry about."

She closed her eyes. If only that were true. If only she had the courage to end the charade. But to end the charade meant an end to everything. And the pain of that was simply too great to even contemplate.

For all those years Alexandra had taken their correspondence, their special communication, almost for granted. Only now, with the prospect of losing that unique intimacy, did she realize fully how important it was to her.

She felt him watching her. When she opened her eyes to meet his gaze, her breath caught. How eerie it was to stare into the eyes of a stranger who at the same instant was so achingly familiar.

Greg was a ruggedly handsome man with just enough imperfections to give his face strength and character. He exuded an air of containment, authority, self-assurance. But Alexandra knew that was only one side of Greg Hollis. She was privy to another, deeper, sensitive side of this man. She knew about his insecurities, his vulnerabilities. She knew that he was lonely and scared. She knew that his father's rejection of him and his wife's betrayal had left lasting scars. But they were scars that could not be seen by the naked eye. And that was a fact Greg guarded fiercely. His cool, in-charge facade was something she knew he counted on.

Tears threatened. If Greg were to find out that the one woman he'd allowed himself to trust, the woman to whom he'd bared his soul all these years, had also betrayed him, it would be devastating for him. And for her.

His eyes probed hers, and she turned away, the wave of despair cresting, breaking over her.

Greg sat down on the bed beside her. Alexandra felt the grip of his strong fingers on her arm. She didn't pull away.

His hold loosened slowly, his fingers moving lightly up under the sleeve of her robe to the crook of her elbow.

"Do you want to talk about what's bothering you?" he asked softly.

She shook her head.

"Are you in trouble?" he persisted.

More than she'd ever dreamed possible.

His eyes searched her face. "Boyfriend trouble?"

Alexandra winced.

Greg nodded knowingly. "Okay, Cassie. I understand."

But of course he didn't. Couldn't.

Alexandra felt so helpless lying there, trembling, inert, listening to the sounds of her thumping heart, her shallow breathing mingled with Greg's.

His palm slid back down her bare arm, down to her fingers. He traced each one.

Alexandra felt suspended in space. An involuntary sigh escaped her lips. The world spun as she closed her eyes.

His hand moved to her hip. She was touched by his delicate tenderness.

"I want to get to know you, Cassie." He stroked her face with his other hand.

She squeezed her eyes shut tighter for a moment, but some force more powerful than reason compelled her to open them and meet his gaze again. They stared into each other's eyes. The silence was filled with a heady anticipation.

His hand caressed her cheek tentatively. Her own hand rose to his, but she had no idea if she meant to caress him or stop him. Greg resolved her ambivalence, stemming her movement with his other hand. And then his head lowered slowly, irrevocably.

She knew then how much she longed for him to kiss her and, at the same time, how terrified she was at the prospect. But she lay there frozen, gripped by a powerful inexplicable force that held her in Greg's spell. She could feel the panic, the insanity of it all, but she remained immobile.

Greg's arms slipped under her, lifting her to him. Her limbs felt oddly disjointed. As the moist heat of his mouth closed over hers, she felt as if her bones were melting. She leaned into him, feeling the thrill of satisfaction as his arms tightened around her.

The feel of his lips on hers sent spirals of electricity through her body. One second her hands were hanging uselessly at her sides; the next they were wrapped around Greg's neck.

It was a soft, tender kiss that melted the panic, even the guilt, from her. He kissed her carefully, exploring her mouth, discovering its curves and hollows. His tongue ran across her teeth. Then he licked her lips.

Twenty-six years old, and she had never in her life been kissed like this. It was extraordinary. It left her reeling....

Dear Greg, You'll never believe it. I finally met the man of my dreams. When he kissed me . . . Oh Greg, your kisses transport me to far-off worlds. Greg, I'm so miserable. It isn't fair. I feel so good at the same time. Oh, Greg, we've always told each other everything. But how can I ever tell you what a mess I've made of it all, my darling Greg?

"Are you okay?" Greg touched the curve of her shoulder as he spoke.

Her eyes flew open. *Don't ask me that*, she begged silently. But then she saw he wasn't expecting an answer.

His hands moved to her hair, his fingers threading through the thick auburn curls, still damp close to the scalp. He wrapped a strand around his finger. Incredible color, weight, consistency. And he found himself oddly pleased that her hair didn't seem to matter to her. No fancy hairstyle. Nor did she wear any makeup to speak of. She didn't need it. She was a real head-turner all on her own—not exactly beautiful, but striking. She exuded an astounding mixture of daring and fragility that was exquisite to behold.

His fingers played in her hair, his eyes gently gazing down at her. But his mind drifted for a few moments. . . .

Dear Alex, Hold on to your hat. I met a woman today. She's really quite incredible. I can't believe my reaction to her. Okay, okay. Part of it is a teenage kind of lust. I never wanted anyone so badly. I have no doubt that I'm probably making a complete ass of myself. It isn't going to be easy; I know that for sure. She's unlike anyone I've ever come up against. A woman with a past, but it's definitely going to take some digging to find out what that past is all about. She's got this baffling mixture of innocence, mystery and sublime sensuality. In simpler language, she's knocked me for a loop. And what's really making me more than a little nervous is . . . it's more than lust. There's something about her. I'm scared, Alex. But what's so strange is I'm not as scared as I know I should be. I'd better watch out. Or maybe it's too late for that.

He could feel her watching him intently, worriedly. He smiled. His hand moved to her back, his thumb pressing up along her spine.

She parted her lips to speak. But Greg didn't want to risk the mood being broken. At this moment he didn't want her to tell him anything that would break the spell.

With his thumb he drew a rough line across her lower lip. And then his mouth swooped down and opened over hers again, his tongue slipping past her teeth until it met her own.

Alexandra could feel a rush of desire sweep over her whole body. If she had been about to speak, Greg's kiss wiped all thought from her mind. This time she kissed him back, passionately.

When he finally drew away, Alexandra heard a ragged breath. She wasn't sure, though, whether it came from her or Greg. At the moment she wasn't sure of anything. The dark, stormy world outside the shaded bedroom had vanished. The world inside was foggy, suspended. She felt exhilarated and miserable at the same time. And when her gaze met Greg's, she saw that he was giving her a significant look.

"This is crazy," he said.

She was surprised to hear the roughness in his voice. Her eyes searched his face, the light slowly dawning. Their kiss had hit him hard, too. That had to be it. The intensity of the encounter had thrown him off balance. She could see it in his face. He was having difficulty maintaining control.

Alexandra found herself smiling. For a moment, anyway, they were on equal ground.

Her smile didn't go over well with Greg. She immediately erased it, but it was too late. She could see the uneasiness spread over his features. And then he got up abruptly from the bed, his jaw muscles flexing agitatedly.

Alexandra fully expected him to turn and flee. She could see clearly now that he'd been as affected by their moment of passion as she had been. Which meant she'd managed to break past that shield of his, however briefly. And no one knew better than Alexandra how anxious that would make Greg. Anxious enough to have him make a beeline out of her life. Without intending it, she'd found the perfect solution to her dilemma.

But it turned out that she didn't know Greg Hollis as well as she thought.

Instead of making a beeline exit, he stood looking down at her. "What is it about you, Cassie?" The roughness in his voice was gone as he studied her.

From a purely objective point of view, and Greg was usually quite objective, he did have an answer to that question. Cassie Phillips was striking, sensual and obviously greatly attracted to him despite some equally obvious ambivalence. But there was something else about her.

His lips curved into a smile as he thought about how different she was from the women he usually spent time with. Meg most recently. She was typical of the type. A cool woman, detached from everything except her ambition, her modeling career. Meg was strong willed, supremely sure of herself, happy to talk about her work, spend some of her spare time with him, then gather her things in the morning and dash off to some glamorous assignment. Everything about women like Meg was predictable. There were no surprises. That made the relationship safe and, at the same time, dispensable. How long had it been since a woman had really startled him? Puzzled him? Filled him with a perplexing feeling that could only be described as awe? But now here was a woman, little more than a stranger, who made his mind spin. If he wasn't careful, it might spin right out of control.

He took a steadying breath. "Get a little sleep. I'll wake you in about an hour and we'll eat if you feel up to it."

She nodded obediently, not having the strength to argue.

When he carefully closed the bedroom door, Alexandra lay on the bed, a feeling of weakness, desire and despair spreading through her.

"Now what?" she whispered aloud in the darkening room, the rain continuing its steady, relentless patter on the windows.

And then she sat up suddenly, as if a bolt of lightning had shot through her.

With everything that was going on, she'd almost forgotten about Cassie. Cassie would be arriving home soon from the beauty parlor. She'd be walking right into the middle of this horrifying charade. Alexandra cringed as she envisioned Cassie's conspiratorial smile. And what if Cassie decided the farce had gone far enough? What if she didn't want to continue playing along? What if . . . ?

A cold sweat broke out on Alexandra's body. She leaped out of bed and started searching for Cassie's phone book on her cluttered bureau. Cassie had mentioned the name of her salon this morning. What was it?

She found the small red address book under a pile of folded lingerie that Cassie hadn't gotten around to putting away. Sitting on the edge of the bed, Alexandra went through each page, praying that the number was listed.

There it was. A Cut Above. Alexandra dialed the number with trembling fingers.

It rang four times before an overworked-sounding female voice came on the line.

"Could I please speak to Cassie Phillips?" Alexandra's voice sounded breathy as she cupped the mouthpiece and pressed her lips to it.

"Cassie Phillips?" the receptionist echoed.

"She had a two o'clock appointment. I'm sure she's still there. She was going to get a body wave." As Alexandra mumbled into the phone, her eyes kept darting toward the closed door, praying Greg wouldn't surprise her with a reappearance before she got through to Cassie.

"Hold on. I'll check. I think she's probably under the heat lamps."

After a pause that felt like an eternity to Alexandra, Cassie's voice came through the receiver.

"Let me guess who it is," Cassie said in an amused voice. "My alter ego?"

"This is no time for jokes," Alexandra snapped, throwing the covers over her head to further muffle the sound of her voice in the room.

"Really? I haven't stopped chuckling myself."

"Cassie, please stop. I'm feeling too desperate to cope with your warped sense of humor at the moment."

"Okay, take it easy. I'm sorry." Cassie sounded vaguely contrite. "So the two of you bumped into each other at the Pierce Gallery, did you?"

"He told you?"

"He told me a few interesting facts. I hope you told him that as far as bosses go, I'm pretty damn flexible."

"I didn't know what to say when he asked me what I did. I haven't felt that tongue-tied since I was ten and the principal called me into his office and demanded I explain just why I socked Tommy Aldrich in the jaw."

"Why did you sock Tommy Aldrich in the jaw?"

"Cassie . . . please!"

"Okay. Sorry."

"The thing is I signed your name in the visitors' book when I went into the gallery. I just thought that if Greg ever happened to scan through it...well, I couldn't use my name. And I never dreamed I'd actually come face-to-face with Greg. But then...there he was...." She paused, hoping Greg had left out that she'd fainted, and decided she felt humiliated enough without telling Cassie herself. "And so," she said slowly, "I was stuck with going along with the charade."

"Is he still at the apartment?"

Alexandra sighed. "He's making me lunch. He thinks I need looking after."

Cassie chuckled.

"Stop laughing, Cass. I don't know what to do."

Cassie was silent for a moment. "What do you think of him?"

Now it was Alexandra's turn for silence.

"He is a terrific catch, Alex."

"I've gone and screwed up a perfect relationship" was all Alexandra could reply.

"It wasn't perfect, kiddo. Perfect is...not having to place a postage stamp on all your feelings. You're a bright lady. You must have figured that out by now."

"I'm too upset to figure anything out."

"Well, what do you want me to do?"

"He thinks you're my boss. I told him you were a fashion designer and that I was your assistant."

"That only qualifies as a partial lie then. I doubt you could be hanged for it."

"Believe me, Cassie," Alexandra said wanly, "the noose is out there just waiting for my neck."

"Alex, tell him the truth. Honesty is the best policy."

"I need your complicity, Cassie, not your homilies."

"How do you think they got to be homilies?"

"I can't tell him the truth, Cass. I can't."

Cassie sighed. "Okay. But I've got to tell you, Alex, I'm lousy at this kind of a thing."

"It will just be for today."

"What happens tomorrow?"

Alexandra hesitated. "I'm going to hop the first plane for San Francisco. It's the only way."

"Yeah ... maybe you're right."

Alexandra rubbed her head. It was pounding so hard that Cassie's voice sounded as if it were coming through an echo chamber. "Can you ... do some errands or something when you leave the beauty parlor? I'll have lunch with Greg and try to figure some way to get him out of here right afterward." She squinted over at the clock on the bedside table. "It's three o'clock now. What time is your date tonight?"

"Jim's coming by at five. We're going to a reception for a new business associate and then out to dinner from there."

"Five o'clock," Alexandra muttered. "And you'll need time to shower and change...."

"Look, I have an idea. I'll go over to my club from here. I can shower there. And actually, I can pick up a cocktail dress downtown to wear tonight. It'll be fun to wear something by another designer for a change. I'll give Jim a ring at work and he can pick me up at the club. That will give you all the time you need to cope with Greg Hollis. And it will save me from having to pretend you're Cassie Phillips."

As Cassie talked, a new thought was racing through Alexandra's mind. A simple solution to the whole problem. But she was a little uneasy about suggesting it to Cassie.

"Alex? Are you still there?"

"I'm here. Would you think it absolutely gluttonous of me to ask you one more favor?"

"Absolutely." Cassie chuckled. "But go ahead. It does give me a certain degree of satisfaction to see you in such a dither."

"Thanks a lot," Alexandra said grumpily.

"I mean, Alex, that until today you always gave the impression of being so competent, so content, so self-reliant."

"I did?"

"Until now I'm sure that Greg Hollis was probably the only living soul to know that Alexandra Yates has her insecurities. And that she can feel helpless at times."

"I guess you're right," Alexandra said thoughtfully. "About Greg. And about me."

"So what's the favor?" Cassie's voice was warm.

"It means dragging your date for tonight into the charade, I'm afraid."

"Jim?"

"I just thought . . . if Jim came here to pick you up—I mean, pick me up as you—then, if Greg were still here, he would see for himself that I'm involved with another man. Greg doesn't like to compete. If he knows there's another man actively in the picture, he'll quit. He's always found it safer to let women go chasing after him."

Cassie laughed. "And I bet they do."

"Most of them," Alexandra said significantly, her free hand pressing her temples to try to still the throbbing.

There was a momentary silence. "Okay," Cassie said finally, "I'll call Jim and ask him."

"Do you think he'll go along with it?"

"Knowing Jim, I'm sure he'll get a kick out of the game plan."

"Well," Alexandra sighed wearily, "I guess that ought to do it then. A couple of hours more, and it will be over."

"There's an old saying, kiddo, that it ain't over till the fat lady sings...."

4

WHEN ALEXANDRA RETURNED to the living room a short while later, Greg was standing in the middle of the room looking like a cool assassin who'd just found his target.

"You're not an assistant to a fashion designer," he stated without preamble.

Alexandra felt dizzy, as if she'd stood too quickly. How was it possible that he'd found her out? She stared at him, unable to say a word.

"Why did you lie to me, Cassie? What was the point?" His tone was sharp, but there was a hint of hurt, or at least disappointment, there.

What was the point? His words echoed in her mind. But if he knew she'd lied, then he knew what the point was. Was he merely trying to put her through some added torture? Not that she could blame him.

But wait. He'd called her Cassie. Not Alex. Cassie. Then he didn't know. She gave him a baffled look.

"Maybe," Greg said, moving in a seemingly aimless fashion across the room, "you were afraid I'd be intimidated."

"Intimidated?" Alexandra's voice was hoarse.

He gave her a slow, careful study, which she found grueling. And then he walked the few extra feet to the drafting table and picked up the sketch Cassie had been working on. He held it out toward Alexandra.

"You're good. You're damn good, Cassie."

"Oh" was all she could manage.

He stared at the bold, red plaid coatdress design so beautifully executed on the paper. Then slowly he raised his gaze to her again.

"I don't get it, Cassie. Why lie?"

Alexandra ran the tip of her tongue around her parched lips. "Does it matter? I guess you're right. I . . . didn't want you to think I was some . . . big-shot designer, that's all. No big deal. Listen, I . . . I completely forgot. I have a . . . dinner date tonight. It's getting late. Maybe we ought to skip lunch. You . . . could take the deli stuff home. I . . ."

"You really are something." Greg's smile was hard, but the edge in his words was even harder. "Who's the dinner date?" He saw Alexandra flinch, her cheeks reddening. He figured part of it was the fever she was running, but part of it was pure discomfort. "Oh, I see." He moved in her direction now, and when he was less than a foot from her, his hard hazel eyes met hers evenly.

They stared at each other for a good ten seconds. "So it isn't a casual date. Is this guy the reason you're so distraught?"

Oh, Greg, Greg, she thought mournfully, *I'm getting myself deeper and deeper into a hole.* But she found herself nodding slowly. "We have our . . . ups and downs," she muttered.

"And I presume this is one of your down times."

"I'm trying to work things out."

Greg's gaze narrowed. "And am I one of the ways you're trying?"

"I don't know what you mean."

"Look, Cassie, I know you're feeling under the weather, but I assume you're not that far under to have forgotten those few hot and heavy moments on your bed."

Alexandra flushed again, more deeply. "It...was just a...kiss." She rummaged in her pocket for a tissue. Her nose was starting to run. Damn, another minute and she'd start hiccuping. Would he remember? she wondered. She occasionally still joked in her letters to him about getting an attack of hiccups when she was really embarrassed.

"It was more than one kiss, but who's counting?" Greg gave her a sly smile.

"I don't know what came over me," she said, knowing how pathetically weak an excuse that was. Of course she knew what had come over her.

"Then I guess we're even."

She looked at him straight on, willing herself not to feel intimidated. "I guess so."

His upper lip lifted slightly in a sneer of amusement. "Okay. So let's eat."

Alexandra stared at him, dumbfounded. "Let's eat? Let's eat? But...but..."

He laughed. "So hungry you're stammering, huh?"

"I thought..." Damn, why couldn't she get one simple, cogent sentence out of her mouth?

"I thought you loved pickles."

She laughed, but she wasn't at all sure why.

"Sandwiches are on the kitchen table."

"I give up," she said with a sigh, crossing to the kitchen.

Greg came up behind her. "Good." His eyes sparkled.

"I really do have a date in a couple of hours."

"I really don't think a woman in your state ought to leave the house tonight. It's still raining, and you're running a fever."

They walked together into the kitchen. "I'll be fine," she said with a determination she certainly didn't feel.

He smiled, holding a chair out for her. She slid into it, and he lingered behind her for a moment, letting his fingers lightly stroke her impossibly beautiful hair.

Finally he took a seat across from her and without pause dug into his thick, juicy pastrami sandwich.

Alexandra merely stared at him. "I can't figure you out, Greg."

He finished chewing the bite. "You sound surprised. Give yourself a little time. Hey, I'm a complex person. It's part of my appeal."

"I'm afraid I can't...spare the time. I'm terribly busy, and then there's—"

"The boyfriend you're having all those ups and downs with," Greg finished for her, taking another bite of his sandwich.

She leaned slightly forward, ignoring her own sandwich. She was too upset to eat. And Greg wasn't helping matters. "Right. The boyfriend I'm trying to work things out with."

Greg waved his sandwich at her, slowly shaking his head as he finished chewing. "Huh-uh." He swallowed. "It's not going to work out."

Alexandra gave him an indignant look. She was almost forgetting this was a purely imaginary problem they were discussing. "And what makes you so sure?"

He grinned. "Didn't you ever hear the saying 'actions speak louder than words'?"

She straightened. "I suppose we're back to that kiss."

"Kisses."

"I thought we weren't counting."

He smiled. There was irony in that smile that threatened to undo Alexandra. "You don't kiss like a woman who's determined to work your love life out with another man."

"It so happens, Mr. Hollis, I'm a complex person, too. You can't figure me out any more easily than I can figure you out."

He speared a piece of pickle and popped it into his mouth. "You're absolutely right."

Alexandra pushed her plate away. "I think I'll go lie down and get some rest before my date arrives."

"What's your date's name?" Greg asked casually, watching her rise.

For a second her mind went blank. She turned away. "It's . . . Jim. Jim's his name." Her brow creased. She sounded as if she'd just gotten an answer right in a quiz contest.

"Jim, huh?"

She whirled to face him, her eyes narrowed. "You don't seem to be taking this very seriously. I happen to be very involved . . . with Jim. He . . . he means a great deal to me. As a matter of fact, we've even discussed marriage." *Oh, Alex, you little fool, what are you doing?* she chastised herself silently.

"Marriage, huh? Now you've really got me curious, Cassie. I'd like to see just what kind of man a woman like you would be thinking of marrying."

"I don't find you amusing, Greg."

"Not all of the time, anyway."

He was so glib, so sure of himself . . . so impossible. And so damnably appealing. This whole affair was terribly dangerous. But on some deep level Alexandra recognized she was feeling a certain added excitement for that very reason. She also recognized that it was a very dangerous feeling to give in to.

"Well, if you're so curious, Mr. Hollis, be my guest. I'll be happy to introduce you to Jim." She whirled back around and strode out of the kitchen.

She was almost at her bedroom door when she realized she'd have to go back into Cassie's room in order not to raise any suspicions. *Smart thinking*, she thought, as she saw Greg standing at the kitchen entrance watching her.

"Wait," Greg said, his tone softer. "Look, I didn't mean to get you all riled up. I guess you...just took me by surprise." He had to smile, amused by his own sense of understatement. Cassie Phillips was rapidly turning his world upside down, and he seemed helpless to do much about it.

Her hand absently went to her brow. The pounding in her head hadn't let up.

"Why don't you postpone working things out with Jim for a couple of days? You're sick. It's pouring outside. Call Jim and ask him to give you a rain check."

"I told you, I'm fine," Alexandra said, but her voice was growing more hoarse and her head simply wouldn't stop drumming. If only she could tell Greg that as soon as he left, Jim would be quickly on his way to meet the real Cassie, and she'd swallow a couple of aspirins and climb immediately into bed.

He walked over to her. "You really do need taking care of, Cassie."

"I've managed perfectly well on my own for years now."

The irony in his smile continued to intimidate her.

"Greg, please let's not make this any harder." Excitement mingled with dread as he cupped her face with his hands.

They stared at each other for several moments. Finally, with a sigh, Greg dropped his hands to his sides. As he stepped back, Alexandra made a beeline for Cassie's bedroom, firmly shutting the door behind her.

Greg stood staring at the closed door. A bemused smile curved his lips.

Dear Alexandra, Where was I? Oh, yes, about this woman. She's really quite impossible. I need some words from the wise. Send them quick . . . or it may be too late. . . .

Alexandra had been lying on the bed for some time, but sleep was impossible, for her whole body ached intensely. She knew she'd have to dress for her supposed date, but every ounce of energy seemed to be rapidly deserting her. Of all the times to come down with a sore throat. She needed her wits about her. She needed to get through this impossible charade.

Dear Greg, Meg was right. You are a difficult man after all. Or at least you're making life difficult, no, impossible, for me. And damn you, why are you suddenly acting unlike any of the ways you described yourself? What happened to that man who never pursued women? Why, of all times, must you suddenly decide to behave so contrarily? And something else you never wrote me about, dear Greg. You have the most wicked grin. If I'm not terribly, terribly careful, it's going to do me in.

She was about to tack on a P.S. to her imaginary letter when she was interrupted by a soft rap on the door. It opened slightly before she had a chance to respond.

Greg walked into the room. "I made you a cup of tea."

Alexandra pulled herself up to a sitting position, demurely fixing her robe securely around her. "Thanks."

"And toast. I guess pastrami and pickles aren't very appetizing when you're coming down with the flu."

She took the cup of tea from his hand while he set the toast on the bedside table. "I'm not coming down with the flu. It's just a cold."

"I still say you ought to stay put for tonight. Isn't Jim an understanding kind of guy?"

"He's very understanding."

Greg stood beside the bed, watching her carefully sip the hot tea.

"So what's the problem between the two of you?"

Alexandra took another sip. "I'd rather not discuss it. It's complicated. And . . . it's difficult to talk about."

He nodded slowly. "Yeah, I understand. It's not always easy to really open up to someone. It takes a lot of time. And a lot of trust. It takes a very special relationship for two people to really be able to remove all their masks."

Alexandra lifted her head. "Have you ever had a relationship like that?"

He didn't answer immediately, but a tender smile lit his face. Finally he met her gaze. "Something like that. It's complicated."

Alexandra smiled. "I see."

He smiled back with a look that said she couldn't possibly. Which only made Alexandra smile more.

"I'll clean up in the kitchen for you. Don't forget to eat that toast."

"Yes, doctor."

He started across the room, only to pause at the door and turn back to her. "By the way, who was that woman who let me into the apartment if she isn't your boss?"

She blinked rapidly, momentarily at a loss for words.

"Cassie?" he persisted.

Why, she moaned silently, *does it keep getting worse?*

"My... agent," she murmured.

"Agent? I didn't know fashion designers had agents."

She didn't, either. It was the first thing that popped into her head. What did he want? Brilliance? She wasn't even sure who she was anymore.

"I'm... thinking of... writing a book. And Ca... Karen is interested in helping me."

He gave her a long, shrewd look. "A book on fashion."

"Of course a book on fashion. What other kind of book would I write?"

There was that wicked smile again. "Oh, I don't know. I thought, maybe, the inside scoop on the life and loves of Cassie Phillips. I bet it would make fascinating reading. You'd definitely have one sale, anyway."

She smiled back wanly. "I'll keep the idea in mind."

She watched his hand grasp the doorknob, and then, as if in slow motion, he released his grip, paused and started toward her.

Alexandra was held fast by his gaze as he came up to her. Without a word he drew her to her feet. The silence in the room reminded Alexandra of watching a motion picture that had been put on a freeze-frame, leaving the characters suspended.

His kiss was as delicate as the petals of a flower against her lips. She allowed it with a feeling of exquisite passivity, an erotic thrill spreading, unbidden, over her skin.

When he drew his head back, she whispered weakly, "You'll catch the flu."

"I thought it was just a cold."

"I could be wrong. It could be more serious."

He touched a finger to her mouth and nodded. "You could be right."

She leaned into him, partly in longing, partly for support. He shifted slightly and cupped her face in his hands, planting a small kiss on the tip of her nose.

"Oh, Cassie. Cassie."

She moved away from him fast and gulped in some air. "I have to . . . det gressed. I mean . . . get dressed."

He laughed softly.

Alexandra's eyelids fluttered shut. He drew her tighter to him, slipping her robe off her shoulders, kissing the smooth, satiny curve of her neck.

"This isn't fair," she said with a moan. "I'm lousy at being tough minded when I'm sick. You're taking unfair advantage of me. I can't think straight, Greg. If you keep this up, I may never have a sane thought in my head again as long as I live."

His strong, tender hands moved down her spine. The robe was slipping further off her shoulders.

"I'm not feeling particularly sane at the moment myself," Greg whispered against her ear. "Fact is, you're driving me crazy."

"We can't let this happen." She lifted her head, her hands finding their way under his shirt to his firm, warm flesh.

"Why not?" He touched her chin, lightly kissing her again, her lips tasting of the honeyed tea and something else, an unquenchable thirst.

The buzzer sounded, its shrill sound startling them both. Alexandra's eyes shot up in alarm. "Jim. It must be Jim. He's early." She'd jerked back from Greg, too stunned for the moment to realize her gaping robe allowed a most tantalizing view, one that Greg, being a healthy, red-blooded man, took full advantage of, before Alexandra came to her senses and pulled it closed.

"Jim." Greg sighed with frustration. "Right. How did I manage to forget about Jim?" He gave her a facetious smile. "Okay, take it easy. You get dressed, and I'll keep Jim entertained until you're ready."

Alexandra sighed. This was all she needed. But there wasn't much she could do about it. "I'll be out in five minutes. Tops."

He studied her thoughtfully for a moment as the doorbell rang a second time. "Aren't you worried that Jim might get a little hot under the collar finding another man here with you?"

Alexandra swallowed hard. "He's not like that. He's not the jealous type."

Greg smiled slyly. "Then the man is a fool."

"Greg, please. The buzzer. Answer it, and let me get dressed."

"Right. The buzzer."

ALEXANDRA'S HANDS were clammy as Jim took hold of them, giving her a warm, affectionate smile.

"Hey, sweetheart, you look terrific." Jim, a tall, lanky man with light brown hair, a smoothly shaven, square face and a strongly nasal New York accent, held her hands out and gave her watermelon-colored, crepe-de-chine dress an approving nod. Alexandra managed a vague smile back. The dress, of course, was Cassie's. As were the makeup, the bone-colored pumps and matching bag. The shoes were killing her. Cassie took one size smaller than she. But she'd be out of them in a few minutes, she thought.

"She does look terrific," Greg observed from a small distance, "but she's probably running a fever of one hundred and two."

Jim, whose back was to Greg, gave Alexandra a conspiratorial wink. "Aren't you feeling well, babe?"

She shot Greg a narrow look before turning her attention back to Jim. "I'll be fine. We can come right back home after dinner."

Jim's smile broadened. "Great idea." He glanced over his shoulder at Greg. "Don't worry about Cassie, Hollis. Now that I'm here, everything's going to be just fine."

Alexandra gave Jim a grateful nod. Truer words were never spoken.

Greg shrugged, his gaze steady on Alexandra. "Well, I guess that's it then." He turned slowly and started toward the door.

Alexandra walked hesitantly over to him. "Thanks, Greg."

He grinned. "My pleasure. Believe me—" he stroked her cheek "—I'll be seeing you."

She shook her head imperceptibly.

He leaned forward, kissed her on the side of her cheek so close to her ear that she shivered at the sensation. Then he smiled with a breezy insolence first at Jim and then back at her. "I'll be in touch."

The phone rang just as Greg walked out. Kicking off her shoes, Alexandra went to get it.

Alexandra's voice was tremulous as she answered. Her eyes were still focused on the shut front door.

It was Cassie on the phone, checking to see if the plan had worked.

"I'm not altogether sure," Alexandra said vaguely.

"What do you mean?"

"It turns out I was wrong about Greg. He's not making any sense."

"He's not making any sense? Hey, kiddo, what about you?"

"I'm not doing much better."

"How did Jim do?"

Alexandra smiled at Jim, who'd walked over to the window and was watching for Greg to exit the building and start down the street.

"Jim was terrific."

Jim grinned. "At last, a woman who appreciates me."

"Tell him I heard that." Cassie laughed over the phone. "And if he wants my appreciation, he'd better hurry on down here."

"He's just waiting until the coast is clear."

Jim gave her a thumbs-up sign. "Tell her I'm on my way." He crossed the room, gave Alexandra a pat on the shoulder and then picked up his raincoat from the clothes tree by the front door.

"Thanks a lot, Jim," Alexandra called out.

"I don't know if it helped any." He winked. "Something tells me that guy Hollis doesn't take no for an answer too easily."

Alexandra sighed. "Something tells me you're right." She gave Jim a small wave as he left.

"Right about what?" Cassie asked impatiently over the phone.

"Cassie," Alexandra said emphatically, "I've got to catch the first plane out of here tomorrow. And I'm afraid you're going to have to play out this charade for just a little while longer. Greg's likely to show up here again, and he's going to wonder why you're at my place...I mean your place. I mean...the thing is I told him you were my literary agent. He saw one of your signed sketches on the drafting table. And naturally he thought it was mine. So now he thinks I'm a big-time fashion designer. Only he's still puzzled about why I told him I was your assistant . . . I mean my assistant. Anyway, I gave him some ridiculous excuse."

Alexandra paused for a quick gulp of air. "And then there's this book I'm trying to put together on fashion. I mean . . . I invented the book. What else could I do? Why would I have a literary agent if I wasn't writing a book? Only I didn't actually say I was writing the book. Just that we—you and I, that is—were talking about it. And, well, if Greg does show up—and I'm pretty damn sure he's going to—well, you can say I had to go off to Paris or Rio or . . . I don't care where you send me. Tell him you're staying at my place because...I don't know...because your apartment is being painted or fumigated or the roof caved in. Oh God, did the roof cave in!"

Tears started running down her face. "I almost forgot. Your name is Karen. It's not a bad name. Really, it was quick thinking on my part. I started to say Cassie, so I didn't have all that many choices."

"Alex, do I get any lines in this part of the play?" Cassie quipped.

Alexandra pressed her lips together for a moment, but she seemed unable to remain silent. "Oh, Cassie, I don't feel good at all. I think I'm coming down with a cold. Now my headache is creeping down the back of my neck. I'm running a fever, and I have to go to bed. Oh, Cassie, I think I'm in love. It's so unfair. And on top of everything, Greg will probably come down with a cold, too. And it will be all my fault because I let him kiss me." The tears were flowing strongly now, and Alexandra squeezed her eyes shut.

"So he kissed you."

Alexandra sighed. "More than once. But who's counting." She started to laugh, the sound bordering on hysteria.

"Look, kiddo, things might feel less awful and less confusing in the morning. Just crawl into bed and forget about it all for now. I won't be home late. If you're still up, we'll talk. But the best thing for you to do is get some sleep. We'll figure something out. If the answer is heading home, we can check flights in the morning. The important thing is to calm down and—"

Alexandra swiped at her eyes with the back of her hand. "I think I've passed the 'calm down' stage. I'm heading straight for oblivion."

"Good girl. Don't let me keep you."

"Cassie?"

"Yeah?"

"You were right."

Cassie laughed softly. "About what? I'm right about so many things."

But Alexandra was dead serious. "About no other man ever measuring up to Greg. From here on out, every guy is going to be second best."

Cassie didn't know what to say.

Neither did Alexandra.

So she simply hung up the phone very carefully and, going into her own bedroom this time, peeled off the borrowed dress and crawled into bed.

Even near oblivion, Alexandra could still feel an awful sensation in the pit of her stomach for what she had set in motion. An aching but pointless apology to Greg hung on her lips.

5

WHEN ALEXANDRA WOKE UP the next morning, she knew she was in no shape to get on an airplane to San Francisco. She wasn't even sure she could get out of bed. She felt as if somebody had sneaked into her bedroom while she was asleep and attached a lead weight to her head. And she didn't need to take her temperature to know she was running a fever.

She felt utterly frustrated by her state of health. She was never sick. Oh, she had the odd cold now and again, but she had no patience with such mundane inconveniences, willing them on their way before they got any kind of meaningful grip on her. Now just when all her other defenses were down, thanks to one Gregory Hollis, her defense against the common cold had deserted her, as well.

She tried to sit up, only to sink back onto her pillow, realizing that the rest of her body felt as weighted down as her head. She squinted in the direction of the clock radio on her bedside table, blinking several times before she accepted that the digital numbers read eleven forty-five. This was the first time she could remember sleeping past eight o'clock in years.

She was making a second useless stab at rising when her door opened and Cassie peeked in.

"You're up."

Alexandra groaned, returning to the relative comfort of her supine position. "That's what you think."

Cassie opened the door fully and walked in. "You really feel lousy, huh?"

"That's a rather optimistic way of putting it."

"Do you want a cup of tea or some breakfast?"

Alexandra grimaced. "No, thanks."

Cassie walked over to the bed and placed a hand on Alexandra's forehead. "You're blazing. I'll get you a cool cloth and then, whether you like it or not, kiddo, I'm phoning a doctor."

"No argument. I know when I'm licked." Alexandra saw the worried look on Cassie's face. "Hey, don't worry. You won't have to play nursemaid—"

"I'd be happy to play nursemaid, Alex," Cassie broke in. "The problem is I won't be able to. I got a long-distance call from Tokyo this morning, and I've got to head out there earlier than I'd planned."

"How early?"

Cassie raised a brow. "This afternoon."

"This afternoon?" Very quickly Alexandra added, "Well, that will be fine. I'm sure the doctor will give me some antibiotics or something and tell me to get a lot of rest. Hearing you cursing under your breath all day as you work on your sketches would only disturb my sleep. And by tomorrow I'll be my old self again."

Cassie grinned. "You're sure about that?"

Alexandra emitted a weary sigh. "I gather you're not referring to my physical state of health."

"Let's recap, kiddo. I want to see if I've got this right. Greg Hollis kissed you . . . how many times? Oh, right, you weren't counting. And what else did you mention to me on the phone? Oh, yes. You're madly in love with him. Well, I could have told you that before you even set eyes on the man. The two of you have been fighting fate for nine years and it's finally caught up with you. Let's see, what else?"

Alexandra did not appreciate the glint in Cassie's eyes. "You want to know what else? I'll tell you what else," she muttered in a scratchy voice. "I've deceived him at every possible turn. I've lied about my name, my address, my profession. On top of everything else, he thinks I'm writing a book."

She sniffed back tears. "But that's not even the worst part. Oh, Cassie, I even lied to him about my love life. Greg thinks Jim and I . . ." She squeezed her eyes shut. "I told him Jim proposed to me." The tears rolled down her cheeks. "If only I'd never walked into that gallery. If only. . . if only I didn't have to be so much in love with him."

"You could tell him the truth, kiddo."

Alexandra's glistening eyes popped open. "Oh, sure. And then what? Cassie, Greg is a proud man. If he knew the truth, he'd feel I'd not only deceived him, but that I'd made a complete fool of him. He'd never forgive me. Never. I know him so well, Cass. That's the problem. I know just how he thinks. I know how vulnerable he is under that cool, glib veneer. I even know that he probably is really crazy about me—I mean the woman he thinks I am—because it isn't like him at all to be in such. . . such hot pursuit. Oh, Cass, if Greg ever finds out the truth, he'll never forgive me. He'd be enraged, hurt, humiliated." Alexandra pressed her hand to her fevered head. "Oh, Cassie," she moaned, "I feel awful."

Cassie squeezed her hand. "I'll call a doctor." She reached for the telephone and dialed information. "Can I have the number of a Dr. George Green on West Sixty-fourth, please?" She glanced over at Alexandra. "Green is the only doctor I know of in Manhattan who still makes house calls. One of my neighbors across the hall uses him and says he's very good."

Alexandra smiled weakly. "I'd settle for a vet right now."

CASSIE LOOKED WORRIED as she spoke to Dr. Green in the living room after he'd finished examining Alexandra.

"I'm glad to hear she'll be feeling a lot better in forty-eight hours, but my problem is I've got to take off by four this afternoon to catch a plane for Tokyo."

Dr. Green, a trim, dapper man with a cheerful manner, smiled reassuringly. "Perhaps you could have someone look in on her every now and then, at least to see to her food. She won't have much of an appetite, but she should try to eat something light three times a day so that she can get her strength back."

Cassie chewed thoughtfully on her lower lip. Then she glanced at her friend's closed bedroom door. "I'll find someone to look after her."

Dr. Green handed her a small sample packet of antibiotics and a prescription for more of the same. "These will last her until morning. If you have time, you ought to have the prescription filled before you leave. Remember, lots of fluids. Perhaps a thermos of water at the side of her bed. And plenty of rest. The more the better. As I told Miss Yates, her throat infection will run its course. She should be feeling a lot better in a couple of days."

Cassie walked Dr. Green to the door and thanked him. After he left, she looked down at the prescription, tapping it with her index finger and then nodding imperceptibly.

Before she went to the corner drugstore, she popped into Alexandra's room to let her know she was going to get the prescription filled. Alexandra was fast asleep, though, and Cassie shut the door softly.

Ten minutes later, the antibiotics tucked in a paper bag, Cassie contemplatively eyed the telephone booth outside the pharmacy.

A wise person, she told herself, never messes in other people's affairs, especially affairs of the heart. Cassie wrinkled her brow. Whoever said she was all that wise? Besides, Alexandra was sick. She needed someone to look after her. Cassie took a resolute breath. A good friend, she decided, was better than a wise friend.

As she flicked through the worn pages of the telephone book to the *H*s, she continued her dialogue with her conscience. Of course, she could call someone other than Greg Hollis. There was Jim and a couple of women friends who might pitch in. But could they give Alexandra—poor, sick Alexandra—the same devoted, loving care that Greg was likely to give her?

GREG ARRIVED at Cassie's front door at five that afternoon. He'd found the key to the apartment in an envelope addressed to him near the mailboxes, just where Cassie's friend and literary agent, Karen, had said she'd leave it for him. He smiled, remembering their brief conversation.

"Cassie's stubborn as nails," Karen had said. "She insists she can look after herself, but she's so weak she can barely crawl out of bed, much less make herself something to eat three times a day. I'd go stay with her myself for a couple of days, but I have a panicked author in Connecticut who's in the throes of a severe writer's block and I've promised to rush out there and spur her on. Anyway, even though I know Cassie will balk, she told me enough about you this morning to convince me she'd be in very good hands under your care."

"What exactly did she tell you this morning?" he'd asked.

"She told me," Karen had answered, "that after meeting you, any other guy was going to be second best. If I were you, though, I wouldn't tell her I told you that just yet."

Greg fit the key into the lock. He turned it tentatively. A hundred times on his way here he'd asked himself if this made any sense. A hundred times he'd told himself it didn't. He'd even written a letter to Alexandra all about his resolve to break things off with Cassie before he got in any deeper.

Dear Alex,

I'm a complete wreck. I've met a woman who is absolutely impossible and absolutely irresistible. This has never happened to me before. I can't think straight. And I can't figure her out. On the one hand, she seems as attracted to me as I am to her, and on the other hand, she seems determined to shove me out of her life. Nothing about her fits any mold I know. She's passionate but unpredictable, strong-willed yet vulnerable as all get-out, seemingly honest one minute and then downright deceitful the next. As baffling as I find her, I find myself continually intoxicated by her. This, my dearest Alex, as you most assuredly know, is not a familiar state of mind for me. Nor is it the least bit pleasant. Once I walked out her door last night—leaving her, I might add (painful as it is for me to recall), in the arms of another man (their relationship but one more source of confusion and bafflement for me)—I resolved firmly to keep on walking. Who needs this? My life is finally running smoothly. No complications. No confusion. Besides, I need to put all of my energy into my work right now. Okay, okay, so I don't like taking too many personal risks. This happens to be a big one. I have a strong feeling I'm going to end up getting burned. I mean, the woman's got me completely off balance. And like you once said yourself, Alex, it's easier to keep your balance when you keep in motion. So, my loyal and caring friend, tell me to pull myself together; tell me I'm doing the smart thing to keep on moving....

Love as always,
Greg

He thought about that letter as his hand rested on the knob of Cassie's front door. Then he thought for the one hundredth time about what he was doing here. A wry smile curved his lips. Who was he kidding? He knew exactly why he was here.

He opened the door to Cassie's apartment and stepped inside. Quietly, so as not to disturb her if she were asleep, he crossed to her room and opened her bedroom door carefully. The room was a study in disorder, everything from lingerie to coats and shoes on the bed—everything but Cassie. His brow creased. Where was she?

He found her in the second bedroom of the apartment. This room was smaller, tidier and the air-conditioning more effective. Maybe that's why, he thought, she'd moved into this room instead of staying in her own. He called her name softly. When she didn't answer, he walked over to her bed and looked down at her, thinking she was asleep until her eyes flickered open briefly.

"Greg?" Her voice was a mere squeak. She looked up at him as though she were still caught up in a dream.

"How are you feeling?"

"What are you doing here?"

"Karen asked me to drop in and check on you."

"Karen?" She looked perplexed.

"It's okay. Go back to sleep. I'll be close by. Call me if you need anything."

She called his name when he was at the door, but when he turned around, she was already fast asleep again.

An hour later, when Greg brought in a piping-hot bowl of aromatic chicken soup and gently woke her, Alexandra pulled the blanket over her head and muttered for him to go away.

A short while later he managed to get her to take her medication. Then he waited until she was sleeping soundly before taking off for the night. He had a pile of work waiting for him at home. Although approval for the Gilrand restoration looked solid, the city hadn't made its final decision. Greg knew that the cost of restoring the estate was making some city managers nervous. Greg had been working with his contractor, Wes Malone, to try to bring the costs down. He hoped there would be a new estimate from Wes waiting for him when he got home.

ALEXANDRA'S KNEES JERKED, and she abruptly woke up from a bad dream. She couldn't remember what it was about, only that Greg was in the dream and they were screaming at each other.

She sat up in bed, conscious for the first time that her awful headache had abated. And her throat was less raw.

As the door to her bedroom opened, she started to call Cassie's name. When Greg's head popped into the room, she gasped.

"What . . . what are you doing here?"

Greg didn't answer. He simply walked into the room and over to her bed. His smile was warm, tender. His hand moved to her forehead, and then his smile broadened.

"Fever's gone," he said pleasantly.

That couldn't be proved by Alexandra. At his touch her whole body seemed to heat up. "Greg?"

"Karen asked me to check in on you. Don't you remember my telling you before?"

"Karen?" Who was Karen? And then, fortunately, her mind cleared. "Oh, Karen. She did?" There was a new edge to her voice. "She shouldn't have done that."

Greg merely smiled as he sat on the side of her bed, very close to her.

"Did she leave already?" Alexandra tried to will her face to stop radiating a heat that had nothing to do with being sick.

"Yesterday afternoon."

Alexandra looked at him in astonishment. "Yesterday. But . . ."

"You've been pretty much out of it for the past twenty-four hours."

"Twenty-four . . ." Her gaze shot to the clock. It was five-thirty.

"How about something to eat?"

Dazed, she turned her head back to face Greg. "You've been here the whole time?"

"I went home for a few hours last night." He grinned. "I bet you're hungry."

Alexandra was still trying to sort out the how's and why's of Greg's presence. "How did you get in?"

"Karen left a key for me downstairs. She was worried about you. I guess you told her enough about me for her to decide I would take good care of you." The hint of amusement in his tone made Alexandra flush. Damn Cassie.

For a long moment they stared at each other, until Alexandra felt herself stretched almost to the breaking point. Before it became intolerable, she muttered, "I am hungry. But I'd like a shower first."

He nodded. "I'd better help you. You're bound to be a little wobbly."

Her eyes widened in mortification. "I'll take my own shower, thank you."

He laughed. "I didn't mean I'd scrub your back, Cassie. Just help you into the bathroom. Unless, of course..."

She gave him a sharp look.

"Okay, okay." He stood up and stretched his hand out to her.

Alexandra was about to refuse it, but as she started to rise, she felt light-headed and grabbed hold of him.

He quickly put his arm around her waist. "Steady. Take a minute to get your bearings."

She gave him a baleful look. How was she supposed to get her bearings when he was practically sweeping her up in his arms, his touch igniting showers of sparks beneath her skin? Despite the cotton nightgown covering her, she felt naked and exposed. "My robe..." she mumbled. She managed to point in the direction of the white wicker chaise near the window.

Greg seemed reluctant to let her go.

"Please . . ." She couldn't get her voice over a whisper.

He smiled resignedly, releasing her slowly, making sure she wasn't going to lose her balance.

When he returned with the robe, helping Alexandra on with it, a bemused smile curved her lips. "I can't believe I really lost an entire day." She hesitated. "I hope . . . I wasn't . . . too terrible a patient."

He turned her around to face him. "You were impossible. You cursed like a soldier and tried to throw a cup of tea at me. You even took a couple of swings at me."

Alexandra looked horrified. "Oh!"

He broke into a smile. "On the other hand, you had a few good moments, too. Like when I got here this morning and you half woke up from a bad dream, insisting I crawl into bed with you and hold you very, very tight."

"I didn't."

"Didn't you?"

"I don't remember . . . anything."

"Well, don't worry about it."

"Easy for you to say."

There was irony in his smile. "While you might not have been the perfect lady, princess, I promise you I was the perfect gentleman." He winked. "I like my women fully conscious when I make a pass."

She grinned, despite herself.

He was standing very close to her. Then he moved perceptibly closer. He was smiling when he kissed her. It was very brief, very tempting. "Just to make my point," he murmured. "Now go take your shower and I'll see to the food."

He left her standing there, body tingling, lips quivering. She felt aroused, embarrassed. Then she started to hiccup and quickly clapped her hand over her mouth. Damn the man.

"I WAS STARVING," Alexandra said with a touch of amazement in her voice as she finished a second helping of chicken soup. "You're a terrific cook."

Greg gave her a curious look. "How'd you know I made it myself?"

"How'd I know?" An easy-enough question for Alexandra Yates to answer. Greg often wrote her about his culinary skills. Soups were his specialty. But Cassie Phillips didn't know that. Cassie Phillips wasn't supposed to know anything about Greg.

Finally she shrugged. "I didn't mean 'cook' in the literal sense. I...I just meant...it was nice of you to heat it up."

Greg continued to study her curiously.

Alexandra smiled back nervously, her hand absently going to her damp hair—springy strands curling with abandon down over her shoulders. "You've certainly seen me at my worst," she muttered, dropping her gaze from his.

He leaned forward. Breaching the narrow distance between them, his hand cupped her chin. "I think you're wonderful looking, Cassie. Even at your worst. And at your best, you're extraordinary."

Alexandra glanced everywhere but at Greg.

"Does that surprise you?" There was devilment in his hazel eyes. His hand dropped to her shoulder, then to the back of her neck. She tried to break free of his grasp, but he slowly shook his head. "I'd better tell you here and now, Cassie Phillips, as much as it is very likely not in my best interest, I do have this very strong desire to figure you out." His smile was tinged with sensuality. "And that's not my only desire, but I bet you figured that part out yourself." His voice was low, husky. He traced a finger down her cheek.

Just as he leaned toward her, his intentions clear to both of them, Alexandra hiccuped. And then she hiccuped again.

Greg stopped moving. He stared at her in complete silence.

Alexandra abruptly pushed back her chair, leaped up and rushed to the sink for a glass of water. She gulped the whole glass of water down, her back to Greg. When she finished, she tried to steady her breathing.

You've really done it now, she chastised herself harshly. Taking a few deep breaths, making sure the hiccups were gone, she forced herself to turn back around and face him.

Greg was studying her with a puzzled expression. Alexandra willed herself to stop trembling.

"That's funny, I almost never get the hiccups. I must have eaten that soup too fast or something," she said in as casual a voice as she could muster.

Greg's continued study and his continued silence began to unnerve her. "What's wrong?" she asked hesitantly.

Greg shrugged. "Just curious, that's all. I know someone on the West Coast who . . ." He changed his mind about finishing the sentence. For some reason he didn't quite understand, he really didn't want to talk about Alex. It was absolutely crazy, but he suddenly felt as if, being here with Cassie, he was cheating on Alex.

It was so ridiculous that he laughed out loud.

"What's so amusing?" Now it was Alexandra's turn to look baffled.

Greg rose and began clearing the table. "Nothing at all. Hey, you'd better get back into bed. Karen told me the doctor said two days of bed rest."

Alexandra's energy was beginning to fade. "I guess you're right." She started across the room, only to pause halfway. "I . . . I didn't really thank you for . . ."

"You don't have to thank me, Cassie. I like looking after you."

"Even though I slugged you a couple of times?"

His eyes sparkled. "Like I said before. There were compensations."

She felt her face heat up and was afraid she'd break into another bout of hiccups. She hurried to the kitchen door, talking very fast as she went. "Well, thanks again. It was very nice of you. I'm fine on my own now. I'm going back to bed. So just call out when you go."

He watched her leave. Then he put the dishes in the sink and leaned on the counter. For all his glib, easy banter with Cassie, he could feel sharp pricks of alarm at the edge of his emotions. Signals telling him to pull out. But all he had to do was look at her, touch her cheek, feel the fiery warmth that mingled with the tentativeness on her lips, and he knew he wasn't going anywhere.

He'd meant what he said about being driven to figure her out. He found himself feeling more like an archaeologist than an architect at the moment, wanting to dig deeper and deeper into the mystery of what made Cassie Phillips tick. He wanted to understand what made her such a mass of contradictions. He wanted to discover her private passions. He was mesmerized by her. He longed to hold her in his arms, inhale the intoxicating scent of her wild hair, her delicate perfume, taste her lips. Even though those warning signals kept right on flashing, Greg felt reckless, willing to throw all caution to the winds. Cassie Phillips was rapidly becoming a dangerous obsession.

WHEN SHE NEXT AWOKE, Alexandra was amazed to find that it was nine o'clock the next morning. She sat up. This time there was no light-headedness. And while her mouth was dry, her throat no longer hurt. She felt whole again, or as whole as one could expect to feel after having gone through an emotional as well as a physical trauma.

The apartment was very still. She got out of bed and reached for her robe. Sunlight streamed into the room. She walked into the living room and looked around, just to make sure Greg had gone. She hadn't heard him leave the night before, but then again, she'd fallen asleep almost as soon as her head had hit the pillow.

She put on a pot of coffee in the kitchen and then went to take a long, refreshing shower. Not bothering with her nightgown when she finished toweling off, she merely shrugged her arms into her robe and opened the bathroom door.

There were two gasps, almost in unison. It was a toss-up who looked more surprised: Greg, standing at Cassie's bedroom door, or Alexandra, fumbling with the tie of her robe at the open bathroom door.

"I thought you'd gone," Alexandra said, feeling instantly weak as she stared at Greg, who had discarded his shirt and wore only his trousers. She was unable to tear her gaze away from his nicely muscled, tanned and naked chest.

"I thought you were still asleep," Greg said at the same time, breaking into a laugh. "I brought some paperwork over with me yesterday and ended up working on it halfway through the night. I thought I'd save myself an extra trip and just sack out on your bed for a few hours. Why'd you switch rooms, anyway?"

His question threw her even more off balance. "I don't know," she muttered with a shrug, managing only with great effort to pull her gaze away from what she easily concluded was the most perfect male body she'd ever seen.

"I borrowed one of your razors. I hope you don't mind." He rubbed his freshly shaven jaw. "Hey, I smell coffee," he remarked cheerily.

Alexandra was still at a loss for words.

Greg didn't seem bothered. He walked across to the kitchen, and Alexandra noticed that he strode in there like a man who'd begun to make himself very comfortable around the place. That made one of them.

Alexandra started toward her room, but Greg was back with two steaming cups of coffee before she got there. "I didn't know if you took milk and sugar."

She shook her head.

"Good. We both drink black coffee, then. Something else we have in common."

Alexandra gave him a curious look. "Something else?"

"We're both designers, aren't we? I design buildings. You design clothes. Very good designs, I might add. I've looked through a couple of your portfolios. I hope you don't mind."

"Actually, I do mind. I'm . . . I'm a very private person, Greg." She set her coffee cup down on a bookshelf and gave him a solemn look, not an easy trick to manage as her gaze kept drifting of its own accord down to that broad expanse of perfect chest. "You really shouldn't have stayed over last night."

"What if you'd had another terrifying dream and wanted someone to hold you again?"

Alexandra swallowed. "But I didn't, did I?"

He set his own cup of coffee down on the end table beside the couch, but he didn't say a word.

Alexandra rapidly felt as if she were having a relapse. She was beginning to feel dizzy and weak again. "Greg, I want you to leave. It's not going to work between us."

"Don't tell me it's because of that guy Jim, Cassie." He started to walk toward her. "Because I don't believe it." He drew inexorably closer. "There was no heat between the two of you. No fire. I would have spotted it." He was close enough now to touch her, but he didn't. "I can feel it between us right now. I could feel the heat, the fire, back at the gallery the moment we met." He smiled seductively. "I just might have passed out myself if you hadn't beaten me to it." He was very close to her now. "What's the point of fighting it, Cassie? Really, what's the point?"

Alexandra gave him a helpless look. For the life of her, just at this moment, she couldn't come up with one single point.

His mouth found hers in a soft, tender kiss. Her lips were trembling. Greg wasn't feeling all that steady himself.

"I'm scared, Greg," she whispered in absolute honesty.

His smile played against her mouth. "Okay, so maybe we've both got our reasons to be scared," he murmured against her parted lips. He drew back slightly, his fingers slipping through her hair, his eyes gently gazing down at her. "I don't think it's wise to give in to our fears."

He slid one arm around her waist. His free hand moved to the tie of her robe.

Alexandra's hand instinctively moved to stop him, but Greg refused to release his grip. As she opened her mouth to protest, he kissed her again, this time pushing his tongue past her teeth. He pulled her against his bare chest, his fingers nimbly undoing the tie around her waist. His hand slipped under her terry robe, stroking the soft, smooth skin of her back, up and down her spine, slowly, intoxicatingly. She could feel him grow hard against her.

Her mind and body were in turmoil. She wanted him to stop. She wanted more. She wanted him to vanish. She wanted him to stay forever. Her body quivered, acting with a will of its own as she pressed into him, all the fight going out of her.

He kept on kissing her, his eyes open, watching her, until her eyes opened, too. His hands moved down her body in smooth, slow, tantalizing circles, his tongue exploring her mouth hungrily, greedily, insistently. Alexandra gave up the struggle completely, his taste filling her with a boneless melting, a fire, a heat . . .

6

A NOT SO FUNNY THING happened on the way to Alexandra's bedroom. The downstairs buzzer sounded. At the sudden sound her muscles jumped, as when a dentist's drill touches a nerve.

"Who's that?" Greg muttered with breathless impatience, reluctantly releasing her.

"I...don't know." She clutched her robe around her, a worried frown on her face.

The buzzer sounded again.

Alexandra bit down on her lower lip. "Let's pretend no one's home. Whoever it is will go away."

Another impatient buzz, this one more drawn out. "It sounds like it's important. I guess you'd better call down and find out who it is." He gave her one of his infamously wicked grins. "Don't worry. I won't forget where we've left off."

Alexandra managed a shaky smile. Not only did this new arrival, whoever it was, complicate matters even more, but the interruption also brought her sharply to her senses. How could she have almost let herself be so thoroughly and so literally swept off her feet? If there was even a chance in a million Greg might ever forgive her, that chance would certainly go up in smoke if they were to make love. For Greg, it would surely be the ultimate deception. And for her, as well. Alexandra tried very hard not to think that it was also bound to be the ultimate ecstasy.

With the greatest reluctance Alexandra went to the hall and pressed the speaker button.

"Yes?"

"Cass? Is that you? It's David. You sound . . . funny. You have a cold?"

Alexandra cleared her throat, casting a surreptitious glance over her shoulder at Greg, who was now sitting on the living-room sofa—out of earshot, she hoped.

"Umm. Yeah. Inflamed throat," she mumbled.

"Hey, I just need to come up for a sec to show you the proofs from last Wednesday's session."

"You . . . you can't." She quickly broke into a fit of coughing. "I'm contagious."

"I'm not worried. Come on, Cass. This is important. I need your input. It'll only take you a couple of minutes."

Alexandra clutched her chest as if the pressure would soothe her pounding heart. If she let this David come upstairs, he'd give her charade away immediately. She was gripped by a cold, choking terror. "Not now, David."

"Cassie, babe, you've never let me down before. This is vital. I told you—"

"I'm just too sick."

"Well, when? I've got to put this package together by this afternoon."

Alexandra couldn't think straight.

After a few tense, silent moments David's frustrated sigh drifted through the speaker box. "Okay, okay. I'll zip down to the studio for a couple of hours and stop by again around two."

"Okay." She felt like a prisoner who'd just gotten a temporary reprieve.

"You really do sound lousy, Cass. I'll bring by some throat lozenges for you when I come back. See you."

She caught a glance at her ashen reflection in the hall mirror. She'd seen healthier faces being wheeled into operating rooms.

Pulse pounding, she steadied herself as best she could and walked slowly back to the living room.

Greg was eyeing her closely as he patted the cushion beside him. "Having some second thoughts?" he asked softly as she ignored his invitation, choosing instead to stand stiffly in the middle of the room.

Alexandra crossed her arms over her chest and clutched her shoulders. "I can't do this, Greg. I can't. I'd never forgive myself. You . . . you don't really know me. I don't . . . know you. I mean . . . we don't know each other. We're . . . we're letting a . . . a simple attraction get . . . out of hand. I'm very involved . . ."

She saw the rueful look on Greg's face. "With my work," she said quickly, knowing it was useless to dredge up Jim again. "I've very involved with my work. And . . . my book. Yes, I can't forget my book. It's going to take a lot of time and energy. I'm going to need . . . my wits about me. This is such bad timing, Greg." If only he knew how bad. Then again, she thanked her lucky stars he didn't. "I can't afford to get emotionally involved right now. Oh, Greg—" she caught her breath sharply "—you'd better go. Believe me . . . it's . . . for the best." Fighting back tears, Alexandra bolted past him to her bedroom.

She was grabbing some clothes from her closet and sniffing back tears when Greg walked in. Alexandra froze as Greg stood there watching her, his hard, lean body poised as if ready to spring. His hazel eyes, which had moments ago been pools of simmering passion, were brimming now with arrogance, frustration and pure masculine stubbornness.

"We'd better have ourselves a little talk, Cassie." The set of his jaw was so grim and angry that Alexandra braced herself against the closet door.

"There's nothing to talk about, Greg."

"Wrong. There's plenty to talk about." His tone was steely.

Even someone who knew nothing about Greg Hollis would know just from looking at him that he was not a man to be easily dissuaded once he'd made up his mind about something. And Alexandra ... Well, Alexandra knew that about Greg better than anyone.

"I don't want to talk about it. Why won't you let it go?" she whispered pleadingly. "This doesn't make any sense."

She wanted to turn away from him, but Greg's brooding gaze compelled her to look at him. There was an almost physical possession in that gaze that made Alexandra's head spin.

"You're right. It doesn't make a lot of sense," he said firmly, hazel eyes darkening. "I don't need this. I've got a lot to contend with in my own life, too. My work, other ... hassles." He began pacing. "Believe me, this isn't ideal timing for me, either. And don't think for one moment that I'm looking for a complicated personal involvement." He kept pacing, but he cast her a wary glance. "Certainly not with a woman who is obviously going through some kind of emotional crisis." He came to an abrupt stop, his eyes slowly drifting with a disturbing intensity down her slender, curved body and then back to her face. "It is crazy. I'm feeling crazy. You're feeling crazy. This whole thing's crazy." This time his voice was lower, huskier.

Alexandra's pulse leaped as Greg walked toward her. Her breathing was shallow and uneven.

He stopped a few inches from her. She could feel his warm exhalations fanning her cheek. She held her breath.

He smiled crookedly. "But you know what's even crazier, Cassie? I keep getting this feeling that we really do know each other, that we seem to be communicating on some other level. It's got me completely baffled. You have me completely baffled."

The color drained from Alexandra's face. She wanted to back away, put some distance between them. But she was held fast by his steady, intense survey.

"You feel it, too, Cassie."

She started to shake her head in denial, but Greg cupped her chin.

"No use denying it. The question is, why are you fighting it so hard? What are you so scared of?"

Alexandra's expression was one of helplessness.

"Are you that scared of involvement? Are you afraid I'll get in the way of your career? Is that it? I saw some of the press clippings on your desk. You're on your way up. If the fashion business is anything like architecture, I imagine it's been a real tough climb to get to where you are. And it's going to be tougher still to fight your way to the top." He smiled. "Funny, but you don't look all that tough. Actually, I'd never have figured you for the fashion business."

Alexandra knew it made no sense at all, but she felt this insane rush of indignation. "I suppose I'm not glamorous enough. Is that it? I don't fit the image. You're used to these cool, chic, sophisticated women—"

His eyes narrowed. "How do you know what kind of women I'm used to?"

Alexandra's mouth went dry. She gave a small, nervous laugh. "A flash of intuition," she said weakly.

The hint of suspicion in Greg's eyes was replaced by one of amusement. "You're right. See? That's what I mean about how we seem to know more about each other than meets the eye. But I'll tell you something you might not have surmised. I'm weary of those cool, vain, ruthless women who reek of expensive perfumes and absolute self-assurance. Nothing really touches them— except maybe money." His features darkened.

"But you've been touched. And hurt." The words were out of Alexandra's mouth before she could stop them.

His expression tightened. "Another flash of intuition?" His voice was hard, sneering.

Alexandra understood perfectly. She'd gotten too close, touched a very sensitive nerve. She could see Greg pulling the protective shield over his face. She could see the harsh lines etched at the corners of his mouth. Just as she could see the vulnerability and the touch of desperation etched even deeper in the shadow of his eyes.

"I suppose that's part of my appeal," she said, at this moment envying those confident, egocentric women Greg scorned. "I don't even own a bottle of expensive perfume. You probably guessed that. And I'm anything but cool and self-assured. I'm sure you figured that out the moment you set eyes on me." She was getting less so by the minute. "And—" she swallowed hard "—sometimes I think I'd be better off being a little tougher, a little greedy. Even a little ruthless." She pressed her lips tightly together as she watched a smile curve his lips.

"Don't look at me like that," she pleaded. She felt dizzy, as if someone had tipped the room at a weird angle. She could hear her breathing grow ragged. "I have to get tough, Greg. I have to start looking out...for my own interests, my...career. I can't let anything... anyone...stop me from doing what's right," she stammered.

As he listened to her speak, Greg's eyes were raking over her luxurious mane of auburn hair, her warm, brown eyes faintly marbled with golden glints, her full, sensual lips; and then his gaze flicked down over her robe, lingering on her breasts until Alexandra's whole body burned.

When he met her eyes once more, Alexandra stopped talking and he gave her a dark, assessing look. With his free hand he smoothed his fingers through his tousled hair. "Look, Cassie," he said softly, "we're both very involved in our careers. Maybe we're both leery of letting ourselves get too involved with a person." He paused, his eyes never wavering from hers. "But I don't think," he said finally in a low, husky voice, "either of us wants it all to end this very moment." His hand moved to her neck and then slowly slid over her throat and down past the opening of her robe. Alexandra's skin burned with his touch.

"No," she said with a gasp, wrenching away, fighting desperately for control. "No. I'm wrong for you, Greg. I'm all wrong for you. Trust me," she pleaded.

Greg could feel his need and frustration choking him. He grabbed her roughly, forcing her back round to face him. "Trust you? How am I supposed to trust you, Cassie, when you never seem to give me a straight answer? Never mind the fact that you're running away from me. You're running from yourself, Cass. You want me to go? Okay, I'll go. But just answer one question first." His large hands pressed roughly into her shoulders. "Do you really want me out of your life, Cassie? Do you really want to let your fears rule you?"

It was really two questions, but Alexandra wasn't about to point that out to him. He looked too angry and defiant as he waited for her reply. Besides, Alexandra could see Greg with her heart as well as her sight. She knew that beneath the hostile facade was a growing hurt and a sense of rejection. She was doing to him exactly what his father had done to him, exactly what his wife had done after less than three years of marriage—casting him aside with the same dishonesty, leaving him to try in vain to make sense out of it all.

Her lips trembled as she sought to come up with a response that would somehow ease his pain. And hers. But she didn't know what she could say. The thought of telling Greg any more lies made her positively ill. The thought of telling him the truth was too awful to contemplate. She was held hostage in a prison of her own making.

"It's more than fear," she admitted. "I can't take the risk. It's too big. It's . . . overwhelming." She looked away, but it didn't make the longing, the desire for him, any less excruciating. "I'm going to be . . . leaving New York very soon. Because of my work. I won't be back for a long time. So you see . . ."

He cupped her chin, forcing her gaze. "What I see," he said with a soft, tender, heart-wrenching smile, "is that we're wasting some very precious time then. Is that really what you want? Or do we listen to our hearts? Do we grab the moment?" His hands left her shoulders and moved possessively down to her waist, drawing her a fraction closer. "Sometimes we're so locked in the future we forget that the future is now. This very moment. I don't want to let the moment go. If I do walk out that door now, that's it, Cassie. I won't, as the saying goes, darken your doorway again. And something tells me, despite all your fears and all of mine, we're both going to regret that more than we regret this...." He gathered her up and kissed her hard on her half-parted lips, pressing her trembling body against him, his heat and desire flicking through her like an incendiary flame.

Dearest Greg, You're right. I can't bear to let the moment go. Not this moment. This precious moment. I'll make it up to you somehow. I love you so.

She was kissing him back hard, absorbing him. They kept on kissing as he slipped her robe off her shoulders. She heard it fall with a gentle swish onto the floor. And then she was naked, in his arms, her body acting with a will of its own.

He placed her gently on the bed. Moments later he was beside her, his strong, muscular, naked body warming her, melting her. It filled her with wonder that she hadn't even any clear recollection of him undressing. It was as though her need for him had jumped leagues ahead of her conscious awareness. In that instant of heated contact Alexandra was lost to all reason, all thought.

She moaned with pleasure as she felt his mouth at her breast, his hands trailing down her rib cage, over the exquisite curve of her hips, one hand dipping between her thighs, stroking, caressing, lingering. Alexandra could feel the pulsing there, his fingers stroking that moist fire.

Alexandra trembled at the erotic onslaught. She saw Greg reach down to his trousers, where they lay on the floor, and retrieve a foil packet from one of the pockets. She stiffened as she heard the rip of the foil seal. But Greg kept caressing her, coaxing her, his touch insistent and yet loving. The flick of his tongue moving back and forth across her nipple drew a moan of pleasure from her lips. She arched up into him, her hands splayed wide over his back.

"Oh, yes, Greg. Yes," she whispered, impulse and passion sweeping over her as she felt his tongue gently, ever so gently, leave a moist trail down her stomach and finally touch the softest core of her. Rasping, urgent sounds escaped her lips. She loved Greg. She'd fought admitting it, but deep in her heart she'd loved him secretly for so many years. And if that love had to remain a secret forever, so be it. She could no more turn back now than she could stop breathing.

Alexandra's fingers curled in his hair, deep shudders erupting inside her. He moved on top of her, his lean, hard body feeling so good, so right. She sighed so deeply with pleasure that Greg looked down at her and grinned that impossible, tantalizingly wicked grin. And then he laughed in a low, sexy way.

Breathless as she was with heady anticipation, Alexandra laughed, too. She felt giddy with laughter. And desire. She pulled his head down to hers and kissed him hard on the mouth, her hands gliding down his back, over his buttocks.

"Our bodies fit perfectly," he whispered hotly against her ear. "Like they were made for each other."

Tears shimmered at the corners of Alexandra's eyes. Her lids lowered, long, dark, moist lashes fanning her cheeks. She sought his lips again, this kiss hungry, urgent.

"You are a little greedy after all." He grinned, pulling back a few inches.

Alexandra's still-moist eyes sparkled. "I'm learning. Do you mind?"

He laughed softly. "No. It feels good. Very good." He stroked her hair, then delicately skimmed his tongue across her lips. "You taste good, too. Incredibly good."

Alexandra touched the back of her palm against Greg's cheek, their gazes locking, his desire speaking to her heart. "This is the moment I've always secretly waited for," she whispered with absolute honesty.

Her eyes fluttered closed as he entered her, time and place evaporating. In that magical, incredible moment nothing in the world existed for Alexandra except the connection they shared. He was her confidant, her very best friend, her soul mate . . . her lover.

She was a sweet blur of sensation as he moved inside her with long, tempestuous strokes. She wrapped her legs around him, her grip as fierce as his, her passion as intense. Her hands were in his hair, tracing the wondrous lines of his face, sweeping across his muscular back, holding him, caressing him, as she began to tremble and explode. She was a sky diver soaring through the air on a perfect gust of wind. She pressed her face into the crook of his neck, her breath, her body held suspended as she soared higher and higher until she was part of the stars, part of the universe.

Greg smiled lovingly, fully giving her those moments of ecstasy. And then the intensity and heat of his own need mounted. He thrust deeply inside her again and again. To Alexandra's astonishment she felt a hot tide of arousal wash over her once more.

They were in perfect sync now, their limbs entwined like a braid of hair, their rhythm filled with a powerful urgency. Greg buried himself in her body, losing himself in her moist warmth, her exquisite beauty. Their bodies fused together as they were transported to that peak of ultimate release.

Afterward Alexandra couldn't move. Couldn't utter a single word. Greg rolled over and sighed, a long, languorous, pleasured sigh. Then he turned onto his side and buried his face in the curve of her neck. He kissed her throat, nibbled her earlobe. When she shivered a little, the air-conditioned coolness that slipped between them chilling her, he pulled her closer, warming her against the heat of his body.

"What happens next?" he whispered, his hands smoothing her wild, tangled hair.

Alexandra couldn't answer. Of course, there was an answer, a simple answer. No . . . not simple at all. Greg had opened a Pandora's box within her and out had tumbled myriad emotions: love, passion, lust, tenderness, desperation, hunger, even greed. How was she ever to squeeze all those volatile, intense, overwhelming feelings back inside?

"Are you sorry, Cass?" He cupped her chin, watching her closely, careful, or so he thought, to hide his fear that her answer would be yes.

Alexandra knew exactly what he was afraid of. She touched his cheek, then let her fingers skim across his temple into his thick, dark hair. "No," she whispered. "It was worth . . . everything." *See, my darling Greg, there are some truths I can share with you.*

He curled up closer to her and kissed her cheek. "So what do we do now?"

Oh, Greg, she thought, *please stop asking such difficult questions.* "What do you want to do?"

"Stay here in bed with you for the rest of our lives."

She laughed softly. "What about your work? Haven't I taken you away from that long enough?"

"I've been keeping tabs on the Gilrand project by phone. Things are going smoothly, knock on wood." He grinned, rapping his knuckles on the oak headboard.

"Oh, Greg, I'd love to see the house sometime," she said without thinking. Common sense hit her a moment later, a rush of thoughts attacking her conscience. *Stop this, Alexandra. You certainly aren't going to be around long enough to visit that house. Tomorrow, come what may, you'd better be on a jet plane to San Francisco. Okay, okay, so you lost control this one time. Okay, it was wonderful, incredible. Greg is wonderful, incredible. He thinks you're wonderful, incredible. Correction, he thinks a woman who lyingly calls herself Cassie Phillips is wonderful, incredible.*

"What's wrong?"

"Wrong?" Alexandra's voice cracked. "Nothing's wrong." She shook herself free of her troubled thoughts. "Tell me more about the Gilrand project, Greg. I want to hear about your work, about you."

Greg stretched his long, muscled limbs, totally comfortable in his nakedness. "Well, the Gilrand Estate's my first major restoration project. Until I landed the contract, I was designing skyscrapers, hotels, shopping malls."

"Did you like that work?"

"Sure." He grinned. "Well, it was big bucks and a lot of prestige. But the truth is it got to be a grind. And I'd always wanted to do restorations. I just got off the track for a while. Anyway, I had to do a lot of wheeling and dealing to land the Gilrand Estate restoration. First they were going to tear the mansion down. Then a few influential people, including my buddy Richard, who owns the Pierce Gallery, got the city to consider funding the restoration. Ten architects competed for the project." He smiled boyishly. "I guess I just got lucky."

"Luck had nothing to do with it, Mr. Hollis. I saw those drawings at the gallery. You're wonderful."

"You mean that?"

She laughed softly and tenderly kissed his lips. "Yes. I mean it. You are wonderful, Greg. Talented. And tender, caring . . . honest." Her fingers absently toyed with the dark mat of hair on his chest. "How come some woman hasn't grabbed you up yet?"

Greg shrugged. "Actually, one did once upon a time."

Alexandra waited, but Greg was silent.

"What happened?" she asked finally, squirming out of his arms and moving to more of a sitting position.

"We got married, then we realized it was a big mistake and we split."

"That's not saying much," Alexandra prodded.

Greg studiously ignored her gaze. "My ex-wife was one of those vain, greedy, egocentric women I kept making the mistake of getting involved with. One day I realized she wasn't going to change, and I packed my bags and bid her a fond but final farewell."

He gave her a quick smile and attempted to get her mind off further questions by provocatively trailing the palm of his hand down the curve of her hip.

But Alexandra took hold of his hand, stopping his exploration. "Are you saying you walked out on your wife?"

Greg merely smiled. "It does happen, Cassie. Don't get me wrong. It wasn't an easy thing to do. I did think I was in love with her. But we were wrong for each other from the start. We wanted different things. We thought differently. Our values, our needs...nothing meshed."

"Was there someone else?" Alexandra persisted.

"For me? No. I'm a regular Boy Scout, Cass. I believe in honesty, integrity and definitely faithfulness."

"And your wife?"

"What?"

"Was she the Girl Scout type?"

Greg's expression hardened for a moment, but he quickly smiled. "She wasn't running around on me, if that's what you're asking. We just didn't get along." His smile broadened. "Why are we talking about my ex-wife? I assure you, she's history."

So, Alexandra thought with a rueful smile, *that's the game you're going to play, Mr. Hollis. And fool that I was, I actually thought one of us here was honest, anyway.* "What about your family, Greg? Father, mother, siblings?"

Greg's expression was slightly cautious, but he shrugged. "I'm an only child. My mother died when I was a kid. There's just my dad."

"What's he like? Are you close?"

Greg cast her a sideways glance. "Pretty close. We get along okay."

"An understanding father. How fortunate you are."

Greg laughed. "I wouldn't go that far." He tousled her hair. "Yeah, he's reasonably understanding."

"He must be very proud of the work you're doing on the Gilrand Estate." Alexandra wondered just how far Greg would go in deceiving her.

"Sure. Sure, he's thrilled. Hey, that's a funny question. Isn't every father proud of his son's accomplishments?" His tone was light, but it didn't hide his growing discomfort with her questions. "Now it's your turn. Tell me more about Cassie Phillips."

"Cassie Phillips," Alexandra echoed. Well, she could tell him about Cassie with relative honesty. "Let's see. She was raised in San Francisco, always dreamed of being a fashion designer, landed a scholarship to the Fashion Institute of Design in New York. Graduated with flying colors. Landed a fashion job in Paris. And in a short time, she'll be off to Japan to introduce her fashions into a chain of boutiques. She intends to be as big a household word as Calvin Klein in a few years."

"You grew up in San Francisco?"

Alexandra looked over at him, and it was suddenly hard to breathe. "Yes. Why?"

"Oh, no reason, really." His fingers began tapping absently on her arm. "I kind of knew someone who lived in San Francisco."

"What's her name? Maybe I know her."

"San Francisco's a big town. It's not too likely." Greg started idly stroking her arm. "I . . . can't even remember offhand."

Alexandra tilted her head. "Not someone you were very close to, then?"

Her questions were making him decidedly uneasy. He knew it made no sense at all not to tell Cassie about Alex. After all, what was Alex to him really but . . . a correspondent, a good friend, a confidante. They weren't lovers. He'd never even set eyes on the woman. Okay, so maybe there'd been a few times—just a few times—when he'd let his fantasies about Alex get carried away. But Cassie was no fantasy. She was real. All right, he was unsure of her. He didn't altogether trust Cassie. And he couldn't begin to guess how things would turn out. All he did know was that he felt incredibly happy at the moment. And he didn't want to do anything intentional to change that. Besides, what would Cassie think if he told her he'd been sharing a uniquely close relationship with a woman for nine years, a woman he'd never set eyes on? And yet this woman was the only person in the world with whom he'd ever risked sharing his deepest, darkest and most intimate feelings. And what, the thought snuck into his mind, was Alex going to think about this sudden mad passion he had for a woman he hardly knew?

"What are you thinking about?" Alexandra saw Greg stiffen. "Tell me." She looked at him straight on, pressing him. Was that a blush she spied rising up that fine, angular jaw?

He was unable to meet her gaze. "Actually, I was thinking about food." Quickly composing himself, he grinned. "I'm starved. How about you? Are you hungry?"

A faint smile curled the corners of her lips. There was a touch of mischief in that smile. She told herself that Greg's deceit didn't condone her own, not by a long shot, but somehow it made her feel slightly better. Who would have ever thought she'd actually feel the least bit cheered by a man lying bald-faced to her? Then again, who'd ever have guessed she'd be in this insane predicament?

"Well?" he asked, puzzled by her amused expression.

"I am a little hungry."

"I know. I still owe you a picnic lunch at the Gilrand Estate. If you feel up to it, I'd love to show you what we're doing there."

Alexandra wanted to be careful about getting pinned down. "Well...maybe it would be better to wait awhile."

Suddenly there was a noise in the living room. Footsteps. A faint cough. Alexandra held her breath. She listened hard. "Who could be out there?" she whispered anxiously.

Greg squeezed her hand. "Stay put." He was grabbing his pants. "I'll go have a look."

As Greg started for the door, a man's voice called out. "Hey, Cass. Are you there? It's me. David. I used the key you gave me so you wouldn't have to get out of bed to answer the buzzer. Hey, Cassie, babe—" there was a light rap on her bedroom door "—are you okay?"

Greg swung the door open, coming face-to-face with a very startled-looking young man.

7

"CASS?" The photographer remained frozen at the open door, his eyes darting from the sheet-covered lump on the bed to the tall, muscular and very angry man zipping his trousers. "Oops. Sorry," he muttered as Greg moved ominously toward him. "I didn't realize—"

"Do you always come breezing into women's apartments without knocking? Or just Cassie's apartment?" Greg's voice vibrated with rage.

David, a slim, natty man of five foot seven dressed in a blue designer jersey, white designer trousers and designer jewelry, raised both hands as if he'd been caught in a stickup. "Hey, buddy, you've got the wrong idea. Tell him, Cass." His voice took on a whine as he found himself staring square into Greg's naked chest.

Alexandra clutched the sheet over her head, remaining breathlessly mute.

"The lady is indisposed, buddy," Greg sneered. "So maybe you'd better do your own explaining."

David was beginning to sweat profusely despite the air-conditioning. "Cassie gave me the key a long time ago when she was going back to Paris. I needed a place to stay while my apartment was being painted. And...I come by every few days or so whenever she's gone to check on the place—that's all. Right, Cass? Will you set your boyfriend straight before he decides to break one of my limbs?"

"Turn around, David," Alexandra mumbled through the sheet.

"What?"

"The lady said turn around." Greg's voice was exaggeratedly patient.

"Yeah...yeah, sure." David turned, facing the door.

Alexandra cautiously peeked out from the sheet. Coughing, sputtering, keeping her hand over her mouth, she muttered, "David's right, Greg. I...I forgot about the key." Another spate of coughing. "Just go, David."

"Hey, you promised, Cass. Just give me five minutes..." Without thinking David started to turn back around.

Alexandra's head shot back under the sheet. "Okay, okay. Wait in the living room for me."

David had backed up a little, but Greg was still close enough for his fist to make contact with the photographer's jaw. Greg was tempted; Cassie's confirmation hadn't been all that convincing.

Before Greg made up his mind, however, the photographer made for the living room in a hurry, shutting the bedroom door firmly behind him.

Slowly Alexandra drew the sheet down from her flushed face. She gave Greg a weak smile. "Terrible timing..." She swallowed. "He *is* telling the truth, Greg."

Greg's gaze narrowed as he eyed her suspiciously. "How many other men have keys to your apartment, Cassie? How many other men do you help out in time of need?"

Alexandra got up angrily, realized she was stark naked and wrenched the sheet off the bed, throwing it around her like a sarong. She stomped over to Greg, tilting her face up to his. "I don't appreciate the implication of your questions, Mr. Hollis." She was seething with indignation, but she had to keep her voice low so that the photographer out in the living room wouldn't hear her unfamiliar voice.

"Well, Miss Phillips, I don't appreciate your open-door policy. I suppose Jim has a key to your apartment, too."

"He does not have a key. If you must know, I...I told Jim the other night that it was over between us. And David is...just a friend. I thought you knew me well enough to know I don't do things like this...casually. But—" her voice caught "—that was stupid of me. You...you don't know me at all."

They eyed each other warily for a few tense moments. Greg's gaze softened first. He even smiled sheepishly. "Okay, Cassie. I'm sorry. I have a short fuse sometimes."

"You certainly do," she retorted. "I never realized how short..." She blanched, shaky hands moving to her face. "I guess I haven't known you long enough to..."

Greg wasn't paying attention to her words. His eyes were focused on the fine planes of her face, a face he was beginning to cherish. His hazel eyes gleamed roguishly, and he reached out and grabbed her, the sheet dropping. He grasped her hands before she could retrieve it.

"Greg, please..." She motioned helplessly in the direction of the bedroom door.

"Say you forgive me first." He leaned his head down abruptly and covered her mouth with his, pulling her slender, luscious body against him.

The kiss was so unexpected, so passionate, that Alexandra was left speechless. All she could do was inanely nod. Then, after the briefest of pauses, she lifted her lips to meet his and kissed him back, her touch soft and tender.

Greg smiled and she managed a weak smile in response.

"I'll forgive you," she said, "if you stay put in here and give me five minutes with . . . David. It's a little embarrassing to . . . explain you to him." She had moved away from Greg as she spoke and bent to pick up her robe. She put it on as she continued. "I mean, he doesn't see me as the kind of woman who . . . who takes a man I hardly know . . . to bed. And—" she was close to the door "—he's right. This isn't at all like me." She stopped talking, stared lovingly at Greg and gave him a beautifully winsome smile. "But I don't feel like we hardly know each other, Greg." She closed her eyes for a moment. When she opened them, she couldn't look directly at him. "I truly don't," she whispered and then, before saying something she would sorely regret, she rushed out the door, careful to close it firmly behind her.

David was sitting on the couch. When he heard the door shut, he sprang up and turned around. "Hey, Cass, I'm really sorry. . ."

Alexandra could readily sympathize with the look of absolute bafflement on the photographer's face when he realized halfway through his apology that he was making it to a complete stranger.

"What the hell is going on?" he muttered.

Alexandra hurried over to him, pressing her index finger to her lips. She took a firm hold of his arm, steering the stunned man toward the front hall. "I know it's a little confusing, David, but you see there's been...a little misunderstanding," she said in hushed tones, praying frantically that Greg wouldn't come popping out of the bedroom in the middle of her explanation.

"It's all very complicated, I'm afraid," she hurried on in low tones practically pushing him in the direction of the hall. "Cassie's not here." She managed to steer him to the front door.

"She's not here? But . . ."

Alexandra placed her hand over David's mouth. "Shh." She motioned over to the bedroom. "I'm a good friend of Cassie's. And . . . I'm kind of incognito at the moment. It's our little secret. Mine and Cassie's. And now yours. She'll explain everything when she gets back from Japan. We don't want anyone else to know. It would be...awkward. Even dangerous." She was unlocking the door, her movements jerky.

"We don't want anyone to know what?" David shook his head. "What could be dangerous? I don't get it."

She patted his shoulder with one hand, opening the door with the other. "See, I told you it was complicated." She used her hand now to gently propel the perplexed man out the door.

He came to an abrupt stop halfway out. "Hey, what about my shots? I needed Cassie to help me."

"You want me to take a quick look at them?" Alexandra asked impatiently, stepping out into the hall and taking David along with her.

"Are you a designer, too?"

Alexandra managed a weak smile. "Well, not really, but . . ."

"Forget it. Just forget it. I swear, lady, you could drive a guy crazy."

Alexandra sighed. "You're not the first man to tell me that."

The photographer stared at her for another moment, shaking his head. Then he turned slowly and headed down the hall toward the bank of elevators. He was still shaking his head. Once he glanced back over his shoulder to see Alexandra waiting by the door—just to see him safely off.

"You're not a model by any chance?"

"No . . . no. Sorry."

"Too bad. I bet you'd look dynamite on film."

One of the elevators stopped, the doors sliding open. David started to enter. But then he thrust his hand out to keep the doors from closing on him. "What's your name, anyway?"

Alexandra had started back into the apartment. She leaned her head out the door. "Cassie Phillips." She winked conspiratorially.

David gave a mock salute and disappeared into the elevator. Alexandra watched the doors slide shut and then stepped back inside the apartment, closed and locked the door and leaned heavily against it. She barely had time to catch her breath when the bedroom door opened and Greg emerged.

"All finished?" He was still naked to the waist, his broad chest gleaming a honey-hued bronze as the afternoon sun streamed through the windows.

Sharp pangs of longing and regret hit Alexandra. "All finished," she whispered back, her expression grim, the sorrow coming through her voice unmasked. *Damn you, Greg. Why do you have to be so incredibly irresistible? Why couldn't you be bald, fat and ugly? Why did I have to behave like such a fool?* She gave a little shudder, already feeling the loss and loneliness—just reward for her deception, she told herself.

"Cassie . . ."

The concern in Greg's voice wrenched her from her tormented thoughts. She quickly manufactured a plucky smile.

His gaze was watchful, but he kept his tone casual. "Let's get dressed. I want to take you with me to the Gilrand Estate. I have to go over there for a short meeting with my contractor, Wes Malone. He's the guy who'll be doing the blood-and-guts work on the building once we get final approval from the city. The historic landmark commission is all for us, but some folks in the mayor's office are losing sleep over all the dollar signs they're seeing. Malone and I keep trying to come up with ways to cut costs. The city wasn't too happy with our last revised estimate, so we're at it again. If Wes is still around, I want to go over a few items with him. But it won't take very long. Then I'll take you on a guided tour of the estate and we'll find a nice quiet spot for a late lunch. After that we'll talk. Really talk, Cassie." He caught the flicker of a frown on her face, even though she was quick to erase it.

Greg could see that Cassie was only half listening to him. With a mixture of frustration and worry he strode across the room to her. "What's the matter, Cassie?" His hand touched her forehead, but her skin was cool. Almost chilled. He took hold of her hands. "What's going on inside that mind of yours?"

Alexandra made an effort to pull herself together, but her nerves were just too taut.

He gripped her firmly by the shoulders. "Cassie, you haven't gotten yourself caught up in real trouble, have you?"

She stared at him, wide-eyed. "You mean like...
What *do* you mean, Greg?"

"If you're in trouble, Cassie, you can tell me what it
is. You know I'll help you. Is that photographer, David, involved? He seemed awfully nervous."

Alexandra smiled wryly. "The poor guy was terrified you were going to wipe the floor with him." She
turned away from him, unable to bear the look of concern and caring in his gaze. "Greg, you've got it all
wrong."

"Do I, Cass? Tell me you aren't scared out of your
wits."

Alexandra swallowed hard. "Look, Greg, you'll just
have to believe me. I'm not in any trouble."

"No?" His smile was leery. "Don't tell me you always
act so tense, so unpredictable. Cassie, listen to me. I
want to help you. But I can't if you won't tell me what's
going on."

Alexandra forced herself to meet his gaze. "You can't
help, Greg. This is something I have to work out for
myself."

"Well, where do I fit in, Cassie?"

She sighed wearily. "I'm...not sure. I can't sort it all
out right now. It's so...complicated." She turned away.
"I need time, Greg. I just need some time. Don't press
it. Please."

She started past him, but Greg caught hold of the
sleeve of her robe. "Okay, Cassie, I'll give you time—
time to know me better, time to trust me. I can be
trusted, Cassie." He smiled ruefully. "We both need
time. It isn't easy for me to trust, either. Or to let myself get too close to anyone. It's a big risk. I took it once
and it was a complete bust. It's so rare for two people
to be absolutely open and honest...." Once again he

found thoughts of Alex popping unbidden into his mind. How easy and uncomplicated their relationship was.

He trusted Alex, as she trusted him. But then, they'd never had to deal with each other face-to-face. It was different with Cassie. He was scared of the intensity of his feelings for her. He was falling in love with her, and he was angry at himself for letting that happen. Cassie had taken him completely by surprise. He'd only known her for a few days, and already he was having fantasies of marrying her, having children with her, growing old with her. But Cassie gave him very little reason to hope. And she certainly gave him little reason to trust. Which is what made it so crazy.

Well, Alex, he thought, *you can't say I'm taking the easy way out now. So go on and have your laugh. The cool, self-contained, play-it-safe-rather-than-sorry Greg Hollis has finally met his Waterloo. And so, my sweet, dependable Alex, you'd better figure out some way to rescue me if I start drowning.*

Alexandra saw the faraway look in Greg's eyes, even though his gaze was still fixed on her. "Greg," she said softly.

He saw her clearly then. Lifting his hands to her hair, he threaded his fingers through the thick, auburn strands. She lifted her head slightly, and his fingers tightened their grip. Alexandra slipped her arms around his waist and pressed her cheek against his shoulder.

"We'll take it slow, Cass," Greg whispered. "We'll give ourselves time."

Tears squeezed past Alexandra's lashes. *Oh, Greg, if only there were time—time to undo the damage; time to change the rules; time to love and be loved. But there is no time.*

As Greg's arms circled her, Alexandra promised herself in no uncertain terms that she would leave first thing the next morning. It hurt terribly to think of how Greg would feel at her simply vanishing like that, but she was afraid to say anything about it, even a lie, afraid Greg would be able to talk her into changing her mind. She was so vulnerable right now. She was so in love with him. Her own needs and desires were engaged in all-out warfare with her common sense, and it would take very little for those feelings to win the battle. But not the war. The war had been lost from the start.

She lifted her head and gave Greg a tender kiss. She knew how baffled and distraught he would be about her disappearance. But Greg would heal. For him, it had all happened so quickly. For him, this would always be a brief, however wildly passionate, affair with a mysterious woman. In time the memory would fade. He would forget her. And there were any number of women waiting in the wings to step in and console the charming, handsome and eligible bachelor.

As for Alexandra, she'd never forget. Nor did she want to, despite the pain she knew the memories would bring. Somehow she would put these incredible love-filled days behind her and pick up the pieces of her life, a difficult task under any circumstances. What made it almost impossible for Alexandra was that she would have to continue her correspondence with Greg as though nothing had changed. And the truth was everything had changed. Nothing in her life would ever be the same. But she would have to bear that burden. She would have to go on as before. Cassie Phillips might be able to vanish into the night, causing Greg anguish and pain. But Alexandra Yates vowed never to do that.

IT WAS A DAY for surprise entrances. When Greg unlocked the ornate wooden door to the Gilrand Estate and opened it, the heavyset gray-haired man standing at the bottom of a sweeping marble staircase in the hallway let out a gasp of surprise that rivaled that of Cassie's photographer friend earlier.

"What are you doing here, Elroy?" Greg's voice was sharp, his surprised expression tinged with wariness.

Before the startled man could answer, another man, this one older and very distinguished looking in a custom-tailored navy suit, stepped out of a room on the right.

Alexandra heard Greg's sharp intake of air and looked from the two men back to Greg, whose expression was now downright hostile.

"A regular reunion, I see," Greg said harshly. "My ex-boss and my father. Okay, why this little gathering?"

"Take it easy, Greg," Stanford Hollis cautioned. He was tall and muscular like his son. His hair was graying nicely at the temples and he wore it fashionably short. His tanned face was handsome, but harder than Greg's face, even though the features were remarkably similar. He smiled, revealing perfectly even, gleaming white teeth. They were so good they might have been false. But they weren't. Only the smile was false. It didn't reach his hazel eyes. When Alexandra looked into those eyes, she thought she could see anger, strain, discomfort. Stanford Hollis, she knew only too well from Greg's letters, was not a man who welcomed confrontations. He always engineered situations so that there was no question that he was in full control.

"Who let you in? Wes Malone?" Greg was not about to hand over the reins.

"Aren't you going to introduce me to your lovely friend?" Stanford said, a definite edge to his voice.

"Not until you tell me what you're both doing here," Greg threw back.

Steve Elroy's ruddy complexion had grown ruddier in the past minute. He made no bones about showing his discomfort. "Wes Malone wasn't here when we arrived. We got a key . . . from the mayor's office. Your father just wanted . . . to have a look around."

"Where do you fit in, Steve?"

Steve didn't answer. Stanford did. "This place hasn't been designated a historic landmark yet, son. You know as well as I do that there are a few investors interested in purchasing the property from the city."

"And that includes you?" Greg's voice was strained.

"Whoa. That's your problem, Gregory. You're always quick to jump the gun. I'm just having a look-see, that's all. A few people I know are curious about the place. After all, a piece of property directly across the street from Central Park is very valuable."

"I, uh, was telling your father that it's an awfully small lot for . . . any kind of major . . . development," Steve said, clearing his throat nervously.

Alexandra, who'd remained discreetly in the background, gave Elroy a sharp glance and then stared at Stanford. "You don't mean raze the mansion? Why, that would be criminal. There's a great deal of history in this place. I read all about it at the Pierce Gallery where Greg's renderings are on display. Destroying it would be destroying a valuable legacy for the future. Our country has few-enough historic landmarks. And the Gilrand Estate is not only important as a link with our past, it's also an exquisite building. Or at least it will be, once Greg's restoration is complete. For heaven's sake, where's your sense of esthetics?" She stared accusingly at Greg's father.

This time Stanford's smile was more genuine. And more than a touch flirtatious. "Believe me, my dear, I have a great appreciation of beauty and grace." He walked over to her. "Forgive my son's rudeness. I'm Stanford Hollis. And you . . . ?"

"Her name's Cassie Phillips," Greg said sharply. He was as aware as Cassie of the glint of approval in his father's eyes.

"Cassie. A lovely name. A lovely woman," Stanford said, taking her hand and holding it a trifle longer than necessary.

Alexandra felt awkward and uncomfortable. She also felt sorry for Greg. So many times over the years Greg had written her of his father's fierce determination to compete with his son, to guide his every move, every decision. But would Stanford Hollis really go so far as to buy the Gilrand Estate out from under Greg, destroying not only this exquisite building, but his son's dream, as well? Thank heavens Elroy didn't seem very optimistic about the prospect. Alexandra knew that the relationship between Elroy and Greg had been strained since Greg had left Elroy's company, but she had the feeling that the architect wasn't at all happy to be caught in the middle of a possible battle between father and son.

Steve approached Greg. "I caught your show down at the Pierce Gallery. Terrific stuff, Greg. Really. It's clear you've got what it takes for this kind of work."

Elroy's remark did not go over well with Stanford. Nor did it do much to soften the hard lines of Greg's face.

"The boy has what it takes to be one of the premier modern architects in the country," Stanford snapped. "This here—" he made a sweeping gesture with his hands "—is boy's play, Greg. But then, you still are a boy in so many ways."

Greg stiffened. "I'm not the only one who doesn't act his age."

Alexandra had no idea what Greg meant by that remark, but Stanford seemed to find it amusing.

"Like son, like father. At least we have some tastes in common," Stanford said, giving Alexandra a lingering gaze.

Elroy looked nervously at his watch. "Look, I've got a meeting at the office. I'd better . . . get going."

Stanford shrugged. "I'm finished here myself. I'll give you a lift, Steve." He smiled warmly at Alexandra. "You'll have to get Greg to bring you down to Greenwich for a weekend. Any friend of my son's . . ." He let the sentence trail off intentionally, giving Greg a sly smile.

Greg remained sullenly silent as his father gave him a brief pat on the shoulder and exited with Steve Elroy.

There was an almost graveyard silence in the hall after the front door closed. Alexandra didn't know what to say. What she really wanted to do was put her arms around Greg, hold him, love him, wipe out the years of pain his father had caused him. And seemed determined to continue causing.

But Greg looked forbidding, distant. He began walking across the hall, over to an open set of double glass doors on the left. He didn't enter the room, though. He just stood there in the doorway, his back to Alexandra.

"Greg..."

"I don't want to talk about him, Cassie."

With hesitant steps she walked over to Greg. She lightly touched his shoulder. "Okay. Then let's forget about him."

He glanced down at her.

She smiled tenderly.

Ever so slowly a smile curved Greg's lips. "You're quite a woman. You handled him like a charm."

Alexandra's smile deepened. "You handled him pretty well yourself."

He touched her cheek. A tremor ran through her. She tilted her chin up, her lips parted, inviting. As Greg's head lowered, Alexandra saw that the tight lines around his mouth had vanished completely.

The kiss they shared was more tender than passionate; a kiss filled with understanding and compassion.

"You're right," he said, releasing her, "let's forget about dear old Dad. Come on." He swept an arm around her. "I want to confirm your blind faith in this legacy to future generations." He steered her back around to the lavish hallway and then to the front door. "Let's start all over. This hallway is one of the few untouched spots in the building. Oh, it's in disrepair, but the chandelier and all the marble and the fresco work is strictly original."

Alexandra twirled around, taking in the space, the elegantly curved staircase, the huge gleaming crystal chandelier hanging from the frescoed ceiling, the walnut-veneered French doors opening to the drawing room on the left, a great hall on the right.

"I've never been in so grand a place, Greg. I want to see every inch of it, every nook and cranny."

Greg laughed, pleasure eradicating the last vestiges of his upset. He was thrilled by Cassie's excitement. It was so much like his own. "If you think it's something now, wait until we get through with it. Granted, the place is in decay at the moment and we've got our work cut out for us, but Wes Malone and his crew are going to absolutely transform it."

Greg spoke as if the city's okay was a fait accompli. Alexandra was not about to rain on his parade. Greg had told her that day at the gallery that the plans for the restoration had been receiving some wonderful press. Surely there were people out there as powerful as Stanford Hollis who wanted to see the Gilrand Estate attain historical landmark status.

"This place has been uninhabited for years," Greg was saying. "It was left to the city a few years ago, but they never did anything with it. Before that the estate was used as a private school. The building's gone through dozens of renovations, one worse than the other. But when we're done restoring it to its Gothic grandeur, it's really going to be magnificent. Studying the history of the house, doing the research on the original plans, reconstructing the whole thing—it's been the most rewarding work I've ever done. Worth all the hassles, financial sacrifices...worth everything."

Alexandra put her arms around his neck. "Oh, Greg, what a terrific challenge." She kissed him playfully on the corners of his mouth. "Only a man of your exceptional talent, exquisite taste and marvelous vision could do the Gilrand Estate justice."

He smiled down at her, a curious look on his face. How extraordinary that Cassie would be so enthusiastic, so able to understand almost intuitively what doing this restoration meant to him. The only other person he knew who'd been able to share his joy, understand his needs, his drives, his excitement over the project in such a way, had been Alex. Meg, his father, even his colleagues, simply couldn't imagine why he would turn his back on a thriving career that gave him enormous wealth and prestige. He'd been a full partner in Elroy's firm for five years when he walked away. Everyone thought he was crazy. Especially his father. As an exceptionally successful venture capitalist, Stanford Hollis expected his son to uphold certain standards, traditions, a certain image. In his eyes, Greg had failed on all counts, which left an already strained relationship even more strained. Stanford Hollis was not a man who took defeat gracefully. If it hadn't been for Alex's letters filled with support and encouragement over the past few months, Greg knew that he would have been far more greatly affected by his father's disapproval and rejection. As it was, this latest disturbing encounter with Stanford opened old wounds that had never quite healed.

Alex had given him strength and confidence. Now Cassie gave him that and something more. She was real. He could touch her, feel her, hold her. If only he understood what lay at the heart of her anxiety. He pressed her against him very tightly, feeling an incredible sense of oneness with her, yet at the same time unable to bury an unbidden feeling of apprehension. Everything about these past few days seemed almost a fantasy. He didn't trust it any more than he trusted Cassie.

A small gasp escaped Alexandra's lips. Only then did Greg realize how hard he was squeezing her. He grinned, easing his hold. "Sorry."

"You have a funny look on your face," she said, noticing for the first time how her voice echoed in the vast and silent space.

He laughed lightly, pushing his worries aside. "I was just thinking," he said, "how lucky I was to walk into Richard's gallery and find you." He gave her his most sizzling grin. "One of these days you're going to tell me just why you fell into a dead faint at my feet."

Alexandra's smile was bittersweet. She raised her eyes to his face, her hand touching his cheek for the briefest of moments. "I'll tell you now. It was that you . . . you reminded me of someone who was . . . very dear to me." She felt tears threatening and quickly turned away.

"Did you love him?" He stood behind her, very close, but not touching.

"Yes, but—" her voice cracked, and she took a deep breath "—he died. It was a long time ago. He . . . he never even knew. At least I don't think he did. Perhaps I never realized just how much I loved him until now." Her voice was a mere whisper.

Greg felt a slow smile spread across his face. He eased her around to face him. "I think I'm beginning to understand, Cassie."

"I'm afraid it would take a great deal of understanding," she whispered, her tears making her voice raspy and spilling down her cheeks. "It . . . it was an impossible love."

"Don't cry, babe," he murmured, circling her waist with his right arm, his left hand brushing a tear off her cheekbone with his thumb.

His words, his tender touch only made her cry more.

He held her close. "I do understand, Cass. More than you realize."

She gazed up at his face, her eyes moist, luminous. "What do you mean?" Her voice was breathy.

He stared down at her. With a trembling hand he brushed a wisp of auburn hair away from her face. "You remind me of someone, too."

"Someone you loved?"

He smiled wistfully. "In a way, yes."

"Your ex-wife?" Alexandra asked tremulously.

He gave a short, derisive laugh. "You most assuredly do not remind me of my ex-wife."

"Then who?" Alexandra persisted, knowing she was courting danger and yet unable to resist it.

He gently cupped her cheeks with both hands and lightly kissed her. "I guess you could say she's a woman who exists more in my fantasy than in reality." He kissed her once again. "There, now everything is crystal clear."

"Is it?" She eyed him with a wry smile.

"No." He grinned. "But we'll work on it. I feel we've made a start." He touched his thumb to her lips. "A very exciting start." He leaned closer, his hazel eyes gleaming seductively.

Alexandra felt a rush of nervousness. "What about my grand tour, Mr. Hollis?"

His grin broadened. "Right. My mind must have wandered." He swung his arm around her. "We'll start down here and then proceed upstairs. If the sun isn't too strong, we can have a late lunch up on the roof terrace."

"That sounds nice," Alexandra said softly. Nice and romantic. A whisper of a sigh escaped her throat.

Greg took her hand and led her into the drawing room located to the left of the foyer. He looked around the room and then at her with a boyish enthusiasm that made Alexandra smile.

"Now," he said excitedly, "you'll have to ignore the partitions—when the estate was a school, they used this room for office space. And this—" he guided her over to a surprisingly ordinary-looking mantel "—is nothing like the original. You probably don't recall the sketches at the gallery I did for the new one. Actually, there are a dozen fireplaces throughout the building and only two of them are originals. Those were in the nurseries and are far less spectacular than the others were. Especially downstairs where the detail work was extraordinary, very fanciful, deliciously ornate."

He went on to point out the faded fresco work on the blotched and water-stained ceiling, the elegant remnants of the hand-carved woodwork, the ornately patterned inlaid oak floor that now bore layers of encrusted dirt and dust, the handsome walnut veneer on the few remaining built-in cupboards.

Alexandra ran her fingers lightly over the wood, only to discover with dismay that the veneer came away at her touch.

"That's what's happening to a lot of the wood veneer in the house," Greg said with a sad smile. "The glue deteriorates over time, and there's been little in the way of waxing or polishing to preserve it. My plan is to restore as much of it as we can and then redo the rest as close to the original as possible. We've got some fantastic craftsmen lined up to do the finish work." He grinned. "It's a good thing the city's footing the bill. The restoration is going to cost a small fortune."

Greg led her across the hall to an enormous room the size of a ballroom. There were six pairs of French doors on either side of the room. On one side they opened to the street and revealed Central Park beyond, and on the other side Alexandra could see the once-lush private gardens at the back of the estate.

"I can't believe the city would actually consider tearing this place down," Alexandra said. "It's such a fantastic landmark."

"This is a prime piece of real estate," Greg pointed out. "Actually, the city probably would have sold it off a long time ago if some architectural firm had been able to come up with a skyscraper design that would have passed the city's planning board. Fortunately for me and the other New Yorkers who want to hold on to as many of the city's historical buildings as possible, this particular parcel of land is a tough site to design a large building for, like Steve Elroy said. I admit my father's appearance here today has me a bit worried. But I know Elroy's work. There's no way he's going to come up with a design that will get the board's approval. Whereas I may have to cut a few more corners, but I'm banking on final approval from the city once I submit my next cost estimate. I'm not letting this project get away, Cassie. Things are going too well for me to be pessimistic. In fact," he said, putting his hands on either side of her face, "I'm determined to look at the bright side of things." He leaned forward slightly and claimed her mouth in a warm, persuasive kiss.

When he released her, his smile had disappeared. Desire flamed in his hazel eyes. "Oh, Cassie, I want you so much."

Panic and longing welled in her chest. "Greg . . ."

"I know you want me, too. Whatever else is going on for you, I know that you feel as strong a pull as I do. That's enough for now."

He stroked her hair. She'd worn it loose with just a white ribbon to keep the untamed strands off her face. Greg slipped the ribbon off, letting it fall to the floor.

"There used to be wonderful balls in this room at the turn of the century," he said softly, taking her hand, sweeping his free arm around her waist. He began humming a waltz. "May I have this dance, milady?" For an instant he lowered his gaze to the sweet swell of her breasts, and then he lifted it to her face and smiled.

Alexandra could feel her pulse racing, her heart pounding. How could she deny him a dance? How could she deny him anything? Anything, that is, but the one thing she longed to be able to give him—the truth.

The corners of her mouth trembled as she smiled. "I'd be most honored, kind sir."

He began twirling her around the vast space, humming louder, drawing her closer.

"You hum magnificently, sir." She laughed, feeling a little light-headed as he spun her about.

She closed her eyes, put her head on his shoulder, relaxing fully into his lead.

"I have never had a lovelier partner, milady," Greg murmured into her ear, his warm breath thrilling her senses.

She began to hum with him, louder and louder. And then they both began to laugh. And still they kept on dancing, round and round. Round and round.

Oh, my darling Greg, if only we could go on laughing and dancing and loving forever...

8

THEIR PLANNED LATE LUNCH on the roof of the Gilrand Estate turned into dinner. A spectacular dinner.

"I've heard of room service, Greg Hollis, but isn't this taking that concept a bit far?" Alexandra continued to watch, dumbfounded, as the waiter from the Park Hotel a few doors down set a dinner of Chateaubriand, delicate asparagus tips and tiny new potatoes on the rooftop card table now covered with a gleaming white linen cloth. The delivery service included chilled champagne, wine goblets, a single long-stemmed red rose in a crystal bud vase and even candles in little silver holders.

"Thanks. Tell Miss Sawyer I really appreciate it," Greg said to the waiter, handing him several bills from his wallet.

The waiter smiled at both of them, said, "*Bon appétit*" and left.

Greg helped Alexandra into her chair and then poured them both some champagne. Standing by her, he touched her glass lightly. "Here's to sunsets over Central Park, Cass." And then one more clink. "Here's to us."

It was too much. Greg, the beautiful yet desolate mansion, this impossibly romantic and unexpected dinner. There was even mood music, thanks to a small portable radio. Alexandra felt dizzy, reckless, bewitched.

She tried desperately to get a grip on herself. This wasn't reality. It was a dream. And very soon she would awaken, alone, hurting.

"Just how many women do you wine and dine up here, Mr. Hollis?" Alexandra asked in a teasing tone. "And what about this Miss Sawyer? You and she must share a rather special relationship for you to get this kind of service."

Greg smiled wickedly. "I see you're duly impressed."

"I see you didn't answer my question."

"Questions," Greg corrected, moving his own chair close to hers and sitting down.

"What gives with you and Miss Sawyer, anyway?"

Greg laughed softly. "Miss Sawyer owns the Park Hotel. She's sixty-seven, and she has a special fondness for the Gilrand Estate and for the work I plan to do on it. She also happens to think I'm a pretty hot catch."

"She's right. You do this wining and dining very well." Alexandra's voice faltered a bit. She concentrated on spearing a succulent asparagus tip, but as she guided it toward her mouth, Greg waylaid her hand and slipped the asparagus into his mouth.

"Hey, that was mine."

Greg laughed softly, stabbing a tiny new potato and extending it to her lips as a peace offering.

Alexandra laughed, letting Greg feed her the one bite. "If we go at the whole meal this way," she said, swallowing, "this could take forever."

Greg reached out and stroked her cheek. "Haven't you already figured it out, Cassie? I want it to last forever."

Alexandra's whole body trembled at his touch, but his words stabbed through her. "No," she whispered in a strained voice. "It's impossible."

"Nothing's impossible, Cass." He studied her intently. He wished she wouldn't look so scared, so tense. What was she afraid of? Why did she want to keep erecting barriers? If only he could understand her better. But she continued to be a mystery. A wave of frustration moved through him, but he refused to give in to it. He knew that she was very drawn to him despite whatever it was she was grappling with. He would give her time. She'd come around. She had to. This was one woman he wasn't going to let get away.

"Your food's getting cold," Alexandra said softly. "Or are these kinds of dinners so commonplace to you that you can take 'em or leave 'em?" She tried her best to quip, but her voice came out husky, nervous.

He took her hand. "This is a first, Cass. But you know that already, don't you? You know that what's happening between us is unique, special. It's as though I've been waiting my whole life for you to materialize."

Wisps of hair caressed her cheek in the gentle breeze. Alexandra stared out over the treetops, watching a streak of the most vibrant red splash across the sky just above the trees in the park. It was exquisite, magical. Tears rose unbidden in her eyes.

Greg sensed her anguish even though he didn't understand it. He sliced a piece of the pink, juicy meat and guided it to her mouth. "You need to build up your strength," he murmured.

Alexandra nodded slowly, chewing as a few errant tears slid down her cheeks. Yes, she did need strength. All the strength she could muster. But at that moment she knew with absolute certainty that she'd never gain enough strength tonight. Would tomorrow be too late? Her longing and need only added to her resolve that tomorrow she must flee. But right now, at this moment, tomorrow felt like a lifetime away.

Greg poured her more champagne as she ate. She was relieved that he didn't question her tears or talk anymore about forever. Her blue feeling passed, and Alexandra found herself eating with gusto. The return of her appetite surprised her, but then, everything she did and felt lately surprised her.

She tried to stop Greg from filling her glass to the top. "You're going to make me tipsy," she protested lightly. "But that's the idea, isn't it?"

Greg laughed devilishly. "Exactly."

"Are you going to finish those potatoes?"

Greg stared at her with wonder as he offered her his plate. She slipped the three tiny potatoes remaining onto her own plate and then, after a moment's hesitation, added a few asparagus tips from Greg's plate, as well.

"You're amazing, Cassie."

"Just famished." She winked.

"What goes through that mind of yours? One moment you look like a little girl lost, and the next moment you're the most ravishing seductress I've ever laid eyes on." He pulled her onto his lap as she finished her last bite of food. "You've got my mind whirling, my heart pounding, and my body. . . Oh, Cass, you do the most incredible things to my body."

"I can tell." Alexandra grinned, twisting round to face him better, her movement heating him all the more.

"I want to make love to you again, Cass. I want to explore every inch of your soft, smooth, warm body, every curve, every tantalizing angle." His words were a caress that sent shivers of excitement and longing down Alexandra's spine.

She looked into the beckoning depths of his eyes and smiled alluringly. "What do you say we take a room over at the Park Hotel?"

His eyes sparkled. "I can't wait that long. I'm starving, famished. I have this insatiable craving for dessert."

Alexandra scanned the concrete roof. Not exactly the ideal spot for savoring the kind of dessert Greg had in mind. A dessert she thirsted for as much as he did. She grinned impishly. "I guess we could clear the table."

Greg laughed, a deep and throaty laugh that tingled clear through to Alexandra's nerve endings. He kissed her shoulder, and she could feel the warm vapor of his breath through the thin cotton of her blouse. "I've got a better idea," he whispered against her ear. "But I love your creative thinking."

He rose, scooping her up in his arms. "There are a few nooks and crannies in this house I haven't shown you yet." He captured her lips for an instant, his tongue drawing a wet line across them, leaving her breath shallow, her pulse speeding. "I've been saving the best for last."

He carried her down one flight to the third floor, an area he hadn't taken her through in the grand tour. Down at the end of the hall he paused at a closed door.

"Okay, close your eyes," he ordered with a sweet, tender kiss on each lid.

Alexandra obeyed. She'd already given up all thought of protest. Of any kind. For tonight she was his. For tonight she would claim Greg as her own. There was time for weeping tomorrow.

The door made a small creaking sound as Greg opened it. "Not yet," he warned. "One more moment." He carried her a few more steps. "Okay, now."

Alexandra's eyelids fluttered open. And then she blinked. "Oh my God, Greg, this is wonderful. Unbelievable." She scanned the large loft room whose quaint multi-paned windows looked out over the park. Here was another world, drawn from a time gone by. It had been perfectly, exquisitely restored and furnished in fine antiques. The focal point of the room was a gleaming mahogany four-poster bed.

"Everything here is part of the estate. A lot of the furnishings are long gone, but the city had put the few remaining pieces in storage." He gently released her so that she could move around the room and explore. "A man by the name of Wyeth who's on the historic landmark commission swung it so I could take a few items out of storage to do this one room. While I was working on the renderings for the restoration, I stayed over here most nights. I wanted to really feel what it was once like, soak up the atmosphere."

He walked over to her. "But something was missing. I only realized it now. You fit this room perfectly. A lovely, old-world lass. You could have been Lili Gilrand. Lars Gilrand had this house built for her soon after they married. This very room was her private sitting room. A few pages of her diary were preserved. She wrote about this room being her favorite in the whole house."

"I can see why. The room is large and yet surprisingly intimate. It's partly the garret windows, I think. And all the angles, the feeling of being in a special, secret place. I love it." She draped her arms around his neck.

He slid his hands down over her hips and drew her closer to him, leaving her no doubt of his lusty need.

A reckless, dangerous longing overtook Alexandra. "Make love to me, Greg. Sweep me back in time. For a brief while let me be Lili Gilrand. Let this be our special, secluded, magical hideaway. Let's be lovers, Greg. Hot, passionate lovers. I've never felt more alive than at this very moment."

He stared into her eyes for a long breathless instant. "You've never been more desirable, more beautiful," he murmured huskily, his lips grazing hers.

His kiss deepened even as he guided her to the bed, sinking down with her onto the quilt. Alexandra's heart was beating wildly, her only thought being the way Greg felt against her, how much she needed that sensation.

Greg feasted on her body as he undressed her. His movements were slow, deliberate, his excitement heightened by her shallow breaths, her sighs, her whispered words of pleasure.

He cupped her face, his hands strong yet tender, as he surveyed her. His look was so loving, so full of hope and pleasure that Alexandra could scarcely breathe. Her heart raced. He kissed her lightly as he slipped off her blouse and unfastened her bra.

Pausing in his sensuous task, he half rose and, too impatient to bother with his own buttons, tugged his shirt over his broad shoulders, leaving him naked to the waist. He lifted her then, delicately ridding her of her lacy bra, and then her skirt and panties, finally pressing her warm body to him, her firm, high breasts flattening against his chest, her hard nipples poking into his skin.

She heard the clunk of his shoes hitting the floor, felt his hand slip between them to unfasten his belt and slide down the zipper of his slacks.

"Let me," Alexandra whispered as she hooked her fingers over the waistband, catching hold of his briefs along with his trousers. With a movement as provocative and deliberate as his own, she slowly slid the material down past his hips, past his thighs, until they fell at his feet and he shook them off altogether.

Her open lips moved sinuously down his thighs, taunting, tempting, intoxicating. Greg writhed as if he was on fire. He gasped his desire as her mouth explored him, her hands following the trail of her lips. The sensation was breathtaking for them both.

When he could bear it no more, he drew her up fiercely, his arms fitting tightly around her, his open mouth seeking hers. They shared breaths in a long, fiery kiss, Greg's tongue plunging deep into her mouth.

They couldn't get enough of each other. Greg's hands slid over the smooth, hot skin of her breasts, down along the curve of hip, to the pulsating heart of her.

Alexandra made broken sounds, her lips moving along the warm hollow of his shoulder to his neck, murmuring her pleasure against his hot skin.

"Tell me how good it feels," Greg whispered against her flat belly as his fingers searched out that moist treasured heat deep inside her.

"Oh, Greg, Greg . . . I've never felt so alive, so wonderfully alive. You do the most incredible things to me. Don't stop, Greg. Please . . . don't stop."

"Never, Cassie. Never." His strong hands slipped over her buttocks, lifting her higher. "I'll never let you go."

He planted hot, wet kisses on her stomach, then her breasts. His lips captured one taut nipple, then the other, sucking, tugging, nibbling. He was wild, voracious, and he carried Alexandra with him as they joined in an almost savage dance, first Greg leading, then Alexandra, then Greg again.

She was drowning in divine sensations. She loved the feeling of him deep inside her. Her muscles tightened, trapping him, making him gasp in infinite pleasure. And then, all control gone for both of them, their bodies moved to a turbulent rhythm until they came together in explosively powerful orgasms.

The sun had set and a hazy darkness filled the room, giving it a feeling of heightened unreality. Alexandra lay on her back, sated, exhausted.

"I want this to last," Greg said, breaking the sumptuous silence. And rocketing Alexandra sharply back to reality. "I've felt alone for a long time," he went on. "I spent most of my childhood alone. My father and I never got along. He shipped me off to boarding schools practically before the dirt had been tossed over my mother's grave."

"Greg, don't—"

"I want you to know me, Cass. I want you to understand me. Most of all I want you to trust me."

"I do trust you, Greg. And I think I understand. Just watching you today with your father...I could see your pain and disappointment. But I sensed that your father is hurting, too. My guess is he's as lonely as you."

"He has an odd way of showing it."

"I think he's as fearful of your rejection as you are of his."

He pulled her to him. "You don't know my father."

Alexandra lifted her head, her eyes level with his. "Do you, Greg?"

He smiled at her. "Maybe we've both spent our lives feeling misunderstood by the other. That's not what's important to me right now. I don't want there to be any misunderstanding between you and me, Cass. We have to be honest with each other. You hold so much inside, Cassie. Can't you share it with me? Help me to understand you."

He looked into her eyes, despaired to see the dark anguish there. She tried to smile, but it was painfully bittersweet. He could feel her distancing herself even as they lay naked against each other, having only moments before savored untold heights of passion and love.

"I'm just not ready for this, Greg. I . . . have my career. I'm just . . . on the brink . . . of really making a name for myself. It involves travel, endless work—absolute absorption." She hated the lies, hated herself for saying them. But she felt helpless to say anything else. The truth at this point would be utterly cruel.

"You never talk about your work." Greg's statement was clearly accusatory.

Alexandra understood perfectly. How could a woman who was so caught up in her career never say a word about it? But how could she weave more lies on top of the ones she was already trapped in?

"My work . . . is very personal. I can't . . . talk about it. It's just . . . something I feel inside."

Greg raised himself on one elbow to look down at her. "And when I'm inside you, Cass, what do you feel then? Can you talk about that?"

"Don't, Greg. Don't spoil something wonderful."

"I'm not the one doing that," he said gravely.

Alexandra closed her eyes. *Oh, Greg,* she thought, *what am I going to do?*

As if he could read her mind, he shook his head slowly, stirred to tenderness by the quivering vulnerability of her mouth despite his frustration at her stubborn refusal to open up to him fully. Their lovemaking told him that a part of her wanted that as much as he did. Perhaps he would just have to give her enough breathing space to discover that what they had together had to take precedence over her fashion career.

"We'd better get dressed," she said in a raspy voice.

"Let's stay here the night. No one will bother us. I want to wake up beside you in the morning."

Oh, to be able to do that. Not just tomorrow morning. But every morning. But that was impossible. Look where granting herself one more night had left her. Suddenly she felt desolate, the pain running through her in shuddering waves.

"I have too much work to do. I'm going to be doing a lot of travel and I have to have my designs ready."

"When do you have to leave town?" he asked quietly.

Alexandra hesitated for a moment. "Very soon." Her voice cracked. She rose quickly, gathering her clothes so carelessly scattered about the floor.

"I can catch a cab," she said, dressing hurriedly.

"Don't be ridiculous. I'll take you home." He smiled sadly. "I'll have to cancel those croissants and fresh-squeezed orange juice I arranged with Miss Sawyer to have delivered tomorrow morning from the Park Hotel now." His dark mood had passed. Alexandra recalled what he'd said earlier. He was determined to look on the bright side. She felt his warm, familiar lips teasing the corners of her mouth. "Breakfast would have been so nice, Cass."

"Yes," she said softly. "It would have been."

"Another time." He reached for his trousers and pulled them on.

Alexandra turned away from him as she finished dressing, hiding the tears that burned in her eyes. "Yes, Greg. Another time," she whispered.

9

GREG FOUND A LETTER from Alexandra in his mail the next morning. He hadn't heard from her in over two weeks, his last letter to her having been about his encounter several weeks ago with his father and his breakup with Meg. All of that seemed like a lifetime away now.

He opened the letter, smiling at Alexandra's familiar, direct approach.

San Francisco
July 8

Dear Greg,

I'm worried about you. Reading between the lines of your last letter about your recent encounter with your dad—you know I have a special talent for reading between your lines—I understand how angry and sad it makes you that your father keeps on giving you such a hard time. I also know you are going to deny it once again, but I still say the man is suffering as much as you are. And just like you, he suffers in silence. He just can't reach out, Greg. Maybe he's too old to change his ways. But you haven't reached the doddering stage yet, I hope. So give the old man a chance. Take the first step. Talk to him, Greg. He's a lonely man. He needs you. And you need him.

Now that I've offered my unsolicited advice on that subject, let's get down to brass tacks about your love life. Something tells me, Mr. Gregory Hollis, you engineered Meg's walkout. Come on, buddy. You and I play the same game. We always run scared. What was wrong with Meg? You told me she was beautiful, talented, successful; that you spoke the same language, that you didn't get into each other's hair. Sounds pretty good to me. I doubt she'd keep walking if you gave her half a chance. Maybe you ought to think about it a little more.

And since I'm on a roll, here's another masterful piece of advice. If I were you, I'd be careful about jumping into a new relationship too quickly. My crystal ball, never mind my professional expertise, tells me you're at a very vulnerable stage right now. You've put yourself on the line with your new project, you're trying to block out your feelings about your father, and the woman you've been seeing for six months just walked out on you. If I were you, I'd keep my guard up, take a little time to regroup. I speak, my dearest friend, not only from professional expertise and fortune-telling talents, but from personal experience. As you know, I've stumbled blindly into a few unfortunate relationships myself on occasion. Fortunately, I usually manage to listen to that little warning voice in my head, and I extricate myself pronto. Who wants to end up with their heart in a thousand pieces? Just in case an exit comes along that isn't quick enough, I always keep some Crazy Glue in my back pocket for an instant mending job.

Seriously, Greg, the more vulnerable people are, the rasher they act and the more danger they put themselves in without thinking. So don't go looking for trouble. I really don't think Crazy Glue works all that well on human hearts.

All my love,
Alex

When Greg finished reading the letter, there was an ironic smile on his face. And an almost eerie feeling about Alex's talent at prophecy. It made him decidedly uneasy. He did feel vulnerable, just as Alex said. And he seemed to have done exactly what she had warned him about. Talk about being rash. Talk about danger. Here he was madly in love with a woman who continued to mystify him; a woman who seemed even more afraid of closeness and commitment than he was; a woman, he was still convinced, who was in some kind of serious trouble. He wanted to save her. He wanted to win her. A feeling of weakness and desire welled up inside him. He grew aroused just thinking of Cassie. He kept telling himself things were getting better and that trust would come in time. Cassie might be scared, but she was also passionate, responsive, tender. He just had to take it slow and not scare her off completely. He was determined that Alexandra's prophesy about him ending up nursing a broken heart would not come true. On the other hand, he thought wryly, maybe he ought to pick up some Crazy Glue himself . . . just to be on the safe side.

Greg idly scanned the postmark on the envelope. It was mailed from San Francisco a couple of days after he'd first encountered Cassie in the Pierce Gallery. By this time Alex would probably have received his confused and impassioned letter all about the mystifying Cassie Phillips. No doubt, Alex wouldn't be able to help chuckling over her own fortune-telling talents. It was going just as she'd predicted, all right. *Oh, Alex*, he thought with a rueful smile, *I'm not at all sure I want to see what that crystal ball of yours turns up next.*

He glanced at his watch. It was nine-fifteen. Cassie had promised she'd meet him for lunch at noon. He set the letter from Alexandra down on his drafting table, finished his second cup of coffee and studied the new estimate Wes Malone had dropped off at his apartment last night. It looked good. Real good.

Greg reached across the paper for the phone. He wanted to call the city commission office and let them know right away that he was bringing in an estimate this morning that was a few thousand dollars under the original restoration estimate that those penny-pinchers at city hall had deemed reasonable. Well, they wouldn't squawk now. And by exerting a little pressure, Greg hoped to get a final commitment for a go-ahead before noon. Then he and Cassie could really celebrate in style.

He tried the number several times, wanting to get an early appointment, but he kept getting a busy signal. Frustrated, he slid the estimate sheets into his briefcase and headed out of his apartment.

ALEXANDRA WAS PACKING her suitcase when she heard the downstairs buzzer. Her heart lurched. She glanced at her watch. It was only nine-thirty. It couldn't be Greg, she told herself, walking nervously out of her room as the buzzer went off again. When he'd brought her home last night, he'd insisted on lunch today. But she wasn't supposed to get together with him till noon.

And she'd told him she needed the entire morning to finish up some designs for a deadline, so she'd meet him at Roselli's, a little Italian restaurant just down the street.

"Yes?" There was a nervous tremor in her voice as she depressed the speaker button.

"Federal Express courier. Got a package for you."

"Come in," Alexandra said with relief, depressing the main door opener. She'd arranged with her roommate, Jill, to use a courier to send Greg's letters to her from San Francisco so that there wouldn't be too much time between getting the letters and responding to them. Alexandra did the same, Jill receiving Alexandra's letters for Greg via courier and then mailing them to Greg in preaddressed envelopes that Alexandra had prepared before taking off for New York. It was a rather costly arrangement, but as Alexandra was discovering, it was peanuts compared to the emotional price she was now paying for her foolish deception.

Her handwriting was unsteady as she signed for the thin white mailer. Afterward she took it, unopened, to her bedroom. Stepping around two already packed bags on the floor, she set the mailer on her bed and slowly, methodically continued folding blouses and lingerie and placing them in her suitcase. Her plane left at noon, precisely the time she'd told Greg she'd meet him at Roselli's. She'd called a cab to pick her up at ten-thirty.

After a few minutes she began sniffing back tears and gave up trying to fold her clothes, finishing the task by stuffing them mindlessly into her canvas case. As she struggled to close the zipper of the overstuffed bag, she composed a letter in her head:

Dear Greg, I met the man of my dreams a few days ago. He's sensitive, intuitive, exciting, tender and incredibly sensual. Despite all my best intentions, I seem to have fallen for him like a ton of bricks. And I'm afraid he's fallen pretty hard for me, too. I say afraid because I'm all wrong for him, Greg. He thinks I'm someone I'm not. It's very mixed up. If he ever were to find out the truth about me, he'd be livid. And terribly hurt. I'm certain of that. And so I'm taking the coward's way out. I'm sneaking off. I'm going home. What do you think, Greg? Am I doing the right thing?

Dear Alex, she answered herself, *You've got no other choice.*

She gave up temporarily on the recalcitrant zipper of her suitcase and stared at the courier package. Just as she was about to reach for it, the phone rang.

"Hi," Cassie greeted her cheerily after Alexandra's tentative hello.

"Where are you?"

"In Osaka. But I'm heading back to Tokyo in a few hours. How are you feeling?"

Alexandra grimaced. "Why did you do it, Cassie? Why did you phone Greg and tell him to come over and look after me?"

"What are friends for?"

Alexandra didn't answer.

"I guess I should have minded my own business," Cassie said after a few awkward, silent moments. "Has it been that awful for you?"

"Yes." A pregnant pause. "No." Alexandra sighed. "It's been sheer madness. It's been . . . incredible. And now it's over. I'll be back in San Francisco for dinner." She sat down listlessly on the bed. "I'll feel better once I get there."

"I hope so, kiddo. You sound worse now than when you were in the throes of that throat infection."

"Things could be worse. At least Greg doesn't know the truth. He'll be hurt when he discovers I'm gone, but I don't think he'll be all that surprised. I doubt anything I'd do would surprise him. I've acted so weird since the moment we met. He keeps trying to figure out the cause of my bizarre behavior. He even thought I was in some kind of trouble involving this guy, David, who showed up yesterday to have me—I mean you—look at some photographs he'd done." Briefly she gave Cassie a rundown of her encounter the day before with David.

Cassie broke into laughter.

"I wish Greg had found it so amusing," Alexandra said, unable to hold back a chuckle herself. "He almost broke your friend's jaw."

"Maybe you should have let him believe you were involved with David in some dirty dealings. It would have explained why you'd been acting like such a nut."

"Oh, you don't know Greg. If he did believe that photographer had involved me in anything unsavory, David's bones wouldn't be worth a plugged nickel." There was a brief pause. "By the way, just how many guys do have a key to your apartment?"

"Just David. Sorry about that. I meant to phone him before I left. But my life's been so crazy since I decided to put my designs in a chain of Japanese boutiques. I still wonder if it's worth all the aggravation. I'm not so sure I wouldn't rather be in your shoes right now, even if they are pinching a little."

"A little! Cassie, only a certifiable lunatic would want to be in my shoes right now." She sighed. "Anyway, I'm the one in your shoes—in a manner of speaking."

"Alex, I've never been in love," Cassie said plaintively. "I've never come close to feeling the way you do."

"I've got news for you. It's no bed of roses."

"You do sound as though the thorns are sharp," Cassie admitted.

"I'll be okay. I'll pull myself together. The important thing is to get out now before things get even crazier. Oh, Greg will be upset, all right. And even more baffled then he is now. I know that. But after a while he'll give up trying to figure it all out. Cassie Phillips will no longer exist, and Alexandra Yates will try to undo some of the damage by offering some...pitiful advice, some insipid words of wisdom, some carefully constructed lies."

"Hey, kiddo, you're being awfully hard on yourself. Greg's not the only one who's going to suffer."

"I deserve to suffer," Alexandra retorted harshly.

"Whoa, there. The only crime you committed, the way I see it, is a crime of the heart. You finally realized you were in love with the man who's been your soul mate for nine years. I really do feel for you, Alex."

Alexandra sighed. "Oh, Cass, I used to be able to tell Greg anything. Everything. It used to be so simple." She hesitated, her gaze drifting to the still-unopened package on the bed. "I just got a letter from him via Jill. Now I actually have to build up my courage just to open mail from him. I was trying to steel myself when you called. I'm sure it's all about Cassie...I mean me."

"He's really fallen hard, hasn't he?" Cassie's voice was sympathetic.

"I keep trying to tell myself that he's just attracted to me because I'm so different from the women he usually sees. And that part of it is that I'm not pursuing him. I'm doing the complete opposite, always trying to sneak out back doors. Maybe Greg likes the novelty of being the pursuer for a change." Alexandra groaned. "Oh, who am I kidding, Cass? There's this electricity between us that's so strong we could open our own power plant and supply current for the whole island of Manhattan." She swallowed hard, licked her lips. "Listen, I've got to finish packing. My cab is due here anytime now."

"Alex, keep in touch."

"Yeah . . . sure."

She replaced the receiver in its cradle carefully and stared at the courier package. "You can't be a coward all the time," she muttered to herself. Resolutely she grabbed up the mailer, tore it open and pulled out Greg's envelope. Her movements were less emphatic as she opened that. And downright tremulous as she extracted the letter itself. She read aloud softly:

"Dear Alex,
I'm a complete wreck. I've met a woman who is absolutely impossible and absolutely irresistible. This has never happened to me before. . . ."

She slumped back against the bed, finishing the rest of the letter in silence. "Liar," she said out loud when she was done. "You said you'd pull yourself together, that you'd keep on walking." She tapped the letter hard with her index finger. "Here, right here, you spelled it out. 'I have a strong feeling I'm going to end up getting burned.' Oh, Greg, you should have heeded your own advice, you fool. You shouldn't have waited to hear it from me. Now it's too late, isn't it? Isn't it? You're too far off balance. Oh, Greg, I'm sorry. I'm so sorry."

She crumpled up the letter and stuffed it into her suitcase. Then muttering and cursing, she made another stab at closing the zipper, but to no avail.

Leaving the bag until she calmed down a little, she picked up the other two suitcases and was dragging them out into the living room when the downstairs buzzer gave off a shrill, impatient blast. Alexandra glanced at her watch. It was just ten-thirty. One thing about New York cabbies, they were prompt. As she set down the bags, intending to "buzz" the cabbie in to get them, she told herself that at least her apartment in San Francisco didn't have a buzzer system. If she never heard another buzz again for the rest of her life, she'd be content.

She depressed the button and talked into the speaker. "I'm in apartment 7F. I'll leave my bags outside my front door in the hall. Could you come up and get them? They're kind of heavy."

There was a brief grunt in response as Alexandra pressed the button to let the driver into the downstairs hall. Then she dragged the bags from the living room into the outside hall, closed the door and went back into her bedroom to tackle the last bag.

A disquieting feeling hit her a minute later as she heard the doorbell of the apartment itself ring and she realized that, in her agitation and rush, she'd never even asked the person buzzing from downstairs to identify himself. She could have let in a perfect stranger, a thief. Worse still, she could have let in Greg.

"Hey, lady. Are these all the bags you want me to take?"

At the sound of the deep, Brooklyn-accented male voice coming through the closed door, Alexandra let out her breath in a whoosh, realizing only then that she'd been holding it in like a drowning woman.

"There's one more, but I'll bring it down myself. Take those down and just give me a minute," she shouted.

"Okay, but I'm gonna have to start the meter running."

"Fine. I'm almost ready."

"I'm double-parked out there."

Alexandra frowned. "Well, drive around the block if you have to. I'll be out front by the time you make it once around."

She heard a muttered grunt and then the sound of plodding footsteps heading in the direction of the elevator.

A couple of minutes later, just after she'd finally managed to close the overstuffed suitcase and was giving the bathroom a last-minute check, the doorbell at the apartment door rang again. She froze. It couldn't be the cabbie. She'd checked from the window and seen him put her bags in the trunk. He couldn't get back up here without buzzing her first from downstairs. Then before she could gather her wits, she heard the bolt turn and then the hinges squeak as the door opened.

Panic was replaced by a knowing smile. Cassie's photographer friend, David, no doubt, returning to the scene of the confusion for some kind of a sane explanation. Quite a tall order. Alexandra was still smiling as she stepped out of the bathroom.

"David, is that you?" Alexandra came to an abrupt stop, the smile turning into a grimace on her face. "Greg," she gasped, her brown eyes startled. "Ohhh," she pressed her hand against her chest. "You scared me."

Anger flashed in Greg's eyes. No, more than anger. Rage. Alexandra thought at first it was connected to his having spied her packed bag and put two and two together. But she realized that the bag was still sitting on her bedroom floor out of his view.

"What is it, Greg? What's happened?" Without thinking, she crossed the room to him, gripping his arm. "Tell me."

"They pulled the plug."

Alexandra looked baffled. "What do you mean?"

"I mean that the restoration of the Gilrand Estate has been scrapped. It's over. Finis. It seems a major developer has offered a huge sum of money for the property and presented a design package the planning board approved. It happened late yesterday afternoon. Now do you get it? In a few weeks the Gilrand Estate will be nothing but rubble. It'll be history." He laughed harshly. "Boy, they really made a fool out of me this time." His tone was low and bitter.

"Oh, Greg, you were so sure no one could come up with a design that would pass. Even Steve Elroy said..."

At the mention of Elroy's name Greg's features darkened even more.

"Is Elroy involved, Greg?" And then in a disbelieving voice, "Your father?" Sympathetic tears clouded her eyes as her hand still gripped Greg's shirtsleeve.

But Greg didn't answer. Instead, he silently looked down at her, moved by her caring. As she pressed her head against his shoulder, the flowery scent of her shampoo wafted up to him. It was a scent that made him feel light-headed. Now it stirred a deep ache in him. Today was supposed to have been a day of celebration. And now his new career was crumbling before his eyes. He took in a deep, steadying breath. At least he had Cassie. Her tears touched him deeply. It gave him strength and determination. He still had a few aces up his sleeve. Later he'd explain it all to Cassie. But for now he just wanted to hold her, make love to her, feel her warmth and passion suffuse him. His arm circled her waist. He was just leaning down to kiss her—

The sound of the buzzer stopped his movement.

"Who's that?" he asked with a frustrated sigh.

Alexandra knew it was the cabbie, growing impatient as the minute she'd promised to take getting downstairs had already stretched into several.

The buzzer sounded again. Once, twice, three times. Greg's eyes narrowed.

Without a word—what words were possible?—Alexandra walked past Greg over to the intercom. "I'm coming," she muttered into the speaker.

"We're gonna hit a lot of traffic goin' out to Kennedy. Didn't you say you've got a plane to catch?"

Alexandra was breathing shallowly, her heart pounding. She shot a bleak look over her shoulder at Greg and saw the cold, stark look in his eyes. She quickly pulled her gaze away and fixed it on the intercom. "I'll be right down," she told the driver. Her voice was hoarse but resigned.

A stiff tightness moved across Greg's back, over the features of his face. Alexandra stood by the intercom, frozen for a moment. And then she knew there was nothing else to do but walk by him, get her bag from the bedroom and walk out the door.

Don't look at his eyes, she told herself as she took faltering steps. *Be strong. You're doing this for him, too. It would only be worse later.*

She could feel his harsh gaze compelling her to look at him, face him. Drawn, despite all her efforts, she stopped a few feet from him and looked into those accusing eyes. They bore into her—dark, scornful, mocking eyes. Only Alexandra understood the pain behind them, the sense of awful betrayal he was feeling.

"You're really leaving?" His voice sounded hollow. The corners of his mouth twitched.

"I told you, Greg." Her voice was thin. An aching pain shot through her. If only she'd escaped without this terrible confrontation. She forced herself to continue walking toward the bedroom, blindly, stiffly, with more desperation than determination.

She could feel him glowering at her even as she passed him. And then he was beside her, grabbing her, forcing her around, his look so fierce it frightened her.

"You can't walk out like this!"

"I told you I would be leaving soon." Alexandra winced as Greg's fingers bit into the tender flesh of her upper arm.

Greg let her go. Their gazes met, locked, each reflecting the other's anguish.

Alexandra looked away. "I got a call . . . this morning. It's one I've been waiting for . . . for weeks." She stopped, her breathing so shallow that she felt dizzy. But she had to go on. This was the end of the charade. The last lie. "I've been in negotiation for a . . . big deal. I didn't want to say anything about it because I . . . I wasn't sure it would come through. But it has. I've got to take off for Japan immediately. I'm putting some of my designs . . . into boutiques there. It's a big risk. I've been agonizing over it, really. I've sunk all my money into it. And . . . and I could lose my shirt." She laughed, the sound tinged with hysteria. "I guess I could just design myself another one, right? I am a designer, after all."

Greg didn't find her poor attempt at humor amusing. In fact, his expression didn't change even a fraction.

Nervously Alexandra continued babbling. "I have to go, Greg. I can't do anything about it. I tried to tell you. I tried to explain. I didn't want to run off without a word. But my plane leaves at noon. I was going to write you...."

His features darkened. "I wasn't interested in you as a penpal, thanks. Save your writing for your fashion book." His tone was beyond sarcasm. It was venomous.

Alexandra's eyes burned. So did her stomach, her chest. She couldn't bear Greg's cold fury, his pain. She closed her eyes, but the image of his rage and hurt wouldn't vanish. It flamed inside her head. It would be there for a long time.

"I have to go," she said tiredly.

She picked up her purse from the hall table and then started for the door. He grabbed her wrist.

She tried to pull away, but he wouldn't release his hold. "I needed you," he whispered, more desperation than harshness in his tone. "I've never said that out loud to a woman before." His thumb was pressing into the inside of her wrist. Her pulse was beating wildly.

"Please, Greg," she half moaned, "don't." Her lips trembled with the intensity of her pain.

"I don't believe any of it," he shot at her, watching her closely.

Alexandra went suddenly cold. "What...do you mean?"

"This Japan trip is a red herring. If that hadn't come up, something else would've. You're running because you're scared. You're scared to let yourself love me. Oh, you can mourn that guy you loved who died. That's safe, isn't it, Cass? It doesn't require anything of you. But I'm here. I'm real. And you can't handle that, can you?"

Alexandra merely shook her head slowly.

With a weary sigh Greg dug into his pocket and retrieved the key to Cassie's apartment that Karen had left for him. He tossed it onto the hall table. "I don't know you at all, do I?"

"No. No, I don't suppose you do," she said, struggling to keep her voice steady and her lips from trembling. "Maybe it's better that way."

She took the few necessary steps to the front door. She had to hurry, or she'd miss her plane. She mustn't miss her plane. She mustn't.

She started out the door but stopped, not turning around. "I'm sorry about the Gilrand project, Greg. I'm sorry... about everything." She realized then he never had told her the whole story. Who was the developer? Did Elroy and his father have anything to do with the deal? It would be the final betrayal. She couldn't bear to think it was possible.

Slowly she turned around to face Greg. His expression was grim, detached. She knew he'd never tell her any of the details at this point. "What will you do now?"

He laughed harshly. "I have to go pick up some...Crazy Glue." His eyes narrowed. "Forget it, you wouldn't understand." Almost in a run, he strode past her, nearly knocking her over as he headed for the staircase exit.

She was trembling as she watched him shove the exit door open. In an instant, as the heavy metal fire door swung closed again, he was gone.

"You're wrong, Greg," she murmured, leaning against the doorjamb to Cassie's apartment. "I understand all about Crazy Glue. Only too well." Squeezing her eyes shut, she tried not to cry. A moment later she heard the shrill downstairs buzzer go off again. If she didn't hurry, she might find her luggage on the sidewalk and the cabdriver gone. She was already cutting the time close for catching that plane.

Even as she stepped into the elevator, she thought she could hear the faint sound of that buzzer again. "Hold your horses," she muttered. "I'm in as big a hurry as you are."

An Indy 500 driver couldn't have gotten Alexandra to Kennedy faster than her New York City cabdriver. After a hair-raising race down East Side Drive and the Long Island Expressway, he made it to the airport with fifteen minutes to spare. Alexandra lurched forward as he squealed to a stop at the TWA departure door. He looked around and gave Alexandra a bright smile.

"Well, we made it."

She stared blankly at the man.

"Hey, you okay?"

"What?"

"Look, you better hurry. You don't want to miss your flight, do you?"

She wiped her tear-stained cheeks. Up until now the cabbie had been so intent on making time he hadn't realized she'd been crying—for the whole trip, from the look of her red eyes and sniffles. He felt suddenly sorry for her.

"Man trouble?"

She sniffed. "How did you know?"

"Lucky guess. I've been married three times. I've never seen a woman cry that there hasn't been a man behind it. I was the guy often enough."

"How come?"

"How come what?"

"How come you were married three times?"

"I guess I kept looking for the girl of my dreams."

"Did you ever find her?"

"You find the man of your dreams?" he asked with a sympathetic smile.

Alexandra started crying again. All she could do was nod her head. And then shake it.

The cabbie shrugged. "I get it. You found him, but it didn't work out."

Alexandra blew her nose into her last crumpled tissue. "I've ruined everything. And worst of all, I've hurt him terribly."

"You're not going so good yourself."

"I'll . . . be okay."

"Hey, look, I'm sorry I was so pushy back at your place. Maybe you should have just skipped the cab and given the whole thing a little more thought."

"Maybe," she said in a raspy voice. "I sure couldn't have picked a worse time to walk out on him. His whole career is falling apart. He needs me now. I'm letting him down in every way imaginable."

The cabbie smiled. "Hey, all I gotta do is turn this baby around and head back to Manhattan with you all comfy in the back seat. Simple as pie. A second cab ride's a lot cheaper than plane fare. I'll take it nice and slow going back. Give you a chance to kinda pull yourself together. What do you say?"

Alexandra gave the cabbie a crooked smile. "You're a really nice guy, after all."

"Yeah. My wife tells me that all the time. Big bark but no bite."

"Your third wife?"

He grinned. "The girl of my dreams."

Alexandra twisted the tissue in her hand.

The cabbie watched her agitation. "So what do you say? You don't have more than a couple of minutes to catch that plane. If you're going, you're gonna have to make a run for it."

"And . . . I might miss it, anyway."

"Good chance you might."

She smiled. "I guess there'll be other planes."

"Does that mean we head back?"

Alexandra hesitated for only a moment and then looked the cabbie straight in the eye. "Pull out." She sniffed again. "Oh . . . you wouldn't have an extra tissue around?"

He reached over to his glove compartment and pulled out a travel pack of Kleenex. "Hey, I got tissues, a shoulder to cry on, the gas to get you back to Manhattan. Anything else you need, though, you go talk to that man of your dreams. I bet he'll be glad to help you out."

10

"HELLO, MR. ELROY. This is Cassie Phillips."

"Cassie Phillips?" The voice at the other end of the receiver sounded puzzled.

"Greg Hollis's . . . friend. We met yesterday."

"Yes. Yes, of course. Of course, Miss Phillips. What can I do for you?"

"I'm trying to get in touch with Greg, but his answering service says he's gone out of town. I just saw him a couple of hours ago. I was wondering if you had spoken to him today. Perhaps he mentioned where he was heading."

A sharp, humorless laugh cut her off. "Oh, I spoke to him today, all right. Well, 'spoke' isn't exactly accurate. Let's just say that we had a few words. Greg had more than his share."

"The two of you had an argument? About the Gilrand project?"

"He told you, then."

"Greg told me the project has been scrapped. That the city has decided to sell the property to a developer. He was very upset, as I'm sure you could imagine."

"I guess he's got a right to be. Look, Miss Phillips. Don't get me wrong. I like the guy. I certainly respect his talents. But to tell you the truth, I agree with what his father said yesterday. Greg's career was really taking off here when he got this crazy notion in his head to go into restorations. I tried to talk to him. His father

certainly tried. I'm hoping when he cools down a little..." He breathed thickly into the phone. "You know,
in all the years I've worked with Greg, I've never seen
him lose his cool like that. Something tells me he's got
other problems bugging him, too."

Alexandra sighed. "I think he feels that everyone is
jumping ship on him."

"Oh?"

She wasn't about to go into any details. "Do you
know where I can find Greg? It's really urgent."

"Well, he didn't say, but I have a pretty good guess
where he went from my office."

"Where?"

"To Connecticut."

"Greenwich, Connecticut? To see his father?"

"You aren't thinking of going down there by any
chance?"

"That's exactly what I'm planning to do."

"Let me give you Hollis's number. Maybe you'd better call first."

Alexandra took the number and Stanford Hollis's
address, but she wasn't sure it would be wise to call first.
Greg had been so angry at her earlier he might not want
to see her, even though she'd changed her mind about
leaving just yet.

"I don't think I'll waste time with a call," she said,
more to herself than to Elroy.

"That's not such a good idea."

"Why is that?"

"Let's just say that Greg didn't go down there for a
father-son reunion."

"So Greg's father is behind the Gilrand sale."

"That's not my place—"

"But his father said he was just looking around. He didn't say one word about there being a bid in. And what about what you said? That it would be hard to put up any kind of skyscraper on that lot. My God, you both stood right there and . . . lied bald-faced to Greg!"

A terrible stab of guilt assaulted her. Hadn't she done the same thing? Poor Greg. Deceived at every turn, by everyone close to him.

"It wasn't my place. And I'm sure Mr. Hollis did not want to start a scene with his son. Especially in public. Besides, we didn't know the sale would go through until later in the day. I really did question whether the . . . design would be approved."

"There have got to be dozens of other lots where you can stick a skyscraper. Why there? Why that particular spot?"

"Well, it's a prime location. And it—"

"Stanford Hollis is doing this out of spite. You know that as well as I do. He's determined to kill this for Greg. He just can't bear to see his son cross him."

"I'm sorry, Miss Phillips. My policy is to stay clear of family affairs. I've got a family of my own. That's enough for me to cope with."

"You must realize that this project is very important to Greg's career. His restoration could win him national acclaim. But it's even more important to him personally. Greg is more than an architect. He's an artist. He's a man with a vision. Where is Greg going to stand when the Gilrand Estate is toppled to the ground?"

Steve Elroy hesitated. "I'll tell you where," he said slowly. "He's going to be standing smack dab in the middle of one of his finest creations."

"One of his finest creations? What are you talking about?"

Steve cleared his throat. "Well, I probably shouldn't be telling you all this, but...it's obvious you care a great deal about Greg."

"Tell me what?" Alexandra asked impatiently. "I'm getting confused."

"It's really quite simple. Stanford Hollis is on the board of directors of New Amsterdam Life Insurance. Actually, he's chairman of the board. Anyway, New Amsterdam Life's been looking to put up a new fifty-story office building in downtown Manhattan. Fact is, one of Greg's last projects here was a design for that very building. It was one hell of a design, let me tell you. The best Greg's ever done. He never actually completed it, though, because it turned out the property deal New Amsterdam Life was about to close on fell through. Then a couple of days ago—" Steve paused to clear his throat again "—Hollis—Stanford Hollis, that is—presented the idea of buying the Gilrand property for the skyscraper. I guess the rest of the board went for the idea because they offered really big bucks. And the city was interested. I don't know if you are aware of it, Miss Phillips, but Greg's estimates on the restoration were enormous and there've been a lot of people questioning the advisability—even the feasibility—of going ahead with it. Anyway," he said, after taking another brief pause, "the city wouldn't consider the offer until New Amsterdam came up with a detailed rendering and a set of prints to show the city's planning board."

"And you showed them Greg's design?"

"Not me. This is, not me directly. Stanford Hollis's group handled it all."

"And I suppose the design received the approval of the New York planning board."

"With flying colors. It's custom-made for that spot. Well, it turned out that way, anyway."

"But that design belongs to Greg. You can't—"

"Correction. It belongs to the firm. I have Greg's signature confirming ownership."

"You can't do this to him. It's bad enough to lose the project. But to know that his own building is standing atop the ruins of a dream . . ." Alexandra fought back tears.

"At the time I thought he'd come round about it," Steve said slowly. "The skyscraper's going to be a real feather in his cap."

"Greg doesn't want feathers for designing skyscrapers, Mr. Elroy."

"Yeah, I know. I honestly thought I was doing the best thing for him when I did the finishing touches on that design and concluded the deal with New Amsterdam Life. I suppose Stanford Hollis was a strong influence on my decision. I'll be honest with you, Miss Phillips. Stanford Hollis is a big-time venture capitalist who has his hands in a lot of pies in this town, and he sends an enormous amount of business my way. It's damn hard to turn a man like that down."

"I'd have thought it would be a lot harder, Mr. Elroy, to turn your back on a man you claim to admire and respect," she responded in a clipped, icy voice.

"Ouch." There was an awkward pause before Elroy said, "Listen, Miss Phillips—Cassie—if you see Greg, tell him I'm sorry. If I can undo the damage . . ."

"Yeah, if only it was as easy as that—for any of us," Alexandra said wistfully.

"You're definitely going down to Greenwich, then?"

"Yes. I've got to talk to Greg. Can you imagine how betrayed he must be feeling right now?"

There was another awkward pause. "Oh, I can imagine, all right. As if he and his father didn't have enough to deal with already, if you know what I mean."

Alexandra's brow creased. "I know they've always had a strained relationship. Are you referring to some special issue?"

There was a long pause. "No...no. Nothing special. Look, I hate to cut you off, but I've got a pile of work staring me in the face and it's Friday afternoon. I want to finish up, get out of this place and drown my sorrows at the Hamptons by tonight. Don't forget, tell Greg—" he sighed "—like I said, tell him I'm sorry."

ALEXANDRA'S TRAIN GOT to the Greenwich depot at five. It was a commuter train, the run taking a little more than an hour from Grand Central Station. The train was packed with a full cargo of dressed-for-success business folk, the men sporting well-cut suits and conservative ties, the women in smart, tailored outfits, all of them projecting an air of achievement and wealth. Greenwich was a haven for these rich, successful and weary travelers. The private homes looked like photographs from *Better Homes and Gardens*, the hedges were impeccably groomed, and the town itself was picture-postcard perfect.

It was too bad, Alexandra reflected, that these prosperous suburbanites couldn't do anything about the weather. According to the digital reading on a nearby bank sign, the temperature was ninety-three. Stepping out of the air-conditioned train, the heat wrapped around her like a thick woolen glove.

The cabs lined up outside the depot were filling up fast, and Alexandra had to make a running dash for one of the last ones. Unfortunately, it wasn't air-conditioned. By the time she arrived at the Hollis home ten minutes later, she was damp, windblown and flushed.

At the front door of Stanford Hollis's red brick Colonial-style house, surrounded by old trees, rolling meadow, woods and a perfectly manicured front lawn, Alexandra paused to smooth back her tangled hair and compose herself. Just as she was about to ring the bell, the door opened and she was greeted by a trim, attractive woman in her mid-fifties. She wore a simple gray dress quite close in shade to her neatly cut hair.

Alexandra looked surprised, and the woman smiled pleasantly. "I heard the taxi pull up."

"Oh."

"Can I help you?"

"Actually, I've come to see Greg Hollis. I believe he's here visiting his father." Alexandra noticed the faint look of consternation on the woman's face. "I'm a friend of Greg's."

"I believe Mr. Hollis took a drive into town a short while ago." A flush crept up to her cheeks. "He should be back . . . soon."

"Is Stanford Hollis in?"

There was a brief pause. "Yes."

"May I see him, please?"

Another pause.

Alexandra smiled pleasantly. "My name is Cassie Phillips. I'm a very close friend of Mr. Hollis's son. I'm sure Mr. Hollis won't mind . . ."

Before Alexandra finished her sentence, a tall, very thin blond beauty came up to the door. She wore her hair long with a studied casualness. She had high cheekbones, a finely chiseled nose, large blue eyes and a long, regal neck. She was wearing tennis whites, but

she looked too cool and too composed to have just finished a game. Her only bad point, and there'd be many
who would argue it, was her mouth. Alexandra
thought the mouth stingy.

"Can I help you?" The woman's voice went with her
looks. It was cool, crisp, precise.

Before Alexandra could answer, the woman in gray
replied, "This is Miss Phillips, a friend of Gregory's."

"Oh." The blond beauty gave Alexandra a method-
ical survey before nodding to the woman in gray, who
then slipped off discreetly. "Well, I'm a friend of Greg's,
too. You might say I'm almost one of the family," she
said with a sweet, slow smile, her tone a touch huskier.
"Miss Phillips, did you say?"

"Cassie Phillips. And you're . . . ?"

The woman extended a long, graceful hand, whose
trimmed nails were painted to match the strawberry
sheen of those too-thin lips. "I'm Meg Lincoln." After
the briefest of pauses Meg smiled brightly. "Won't you
come in, Cassie. Greg's gone off in a bit of a huff, but
I'm sure he'll be back after he calms down a bit." As she
spoke, she maintained a grip on Alexandra's hand until she cleared the door and was standing in a bright,
airy foyer.

"You look like you could use a nice, refreshing drink,
Cassie. Why don't I show you to the garden room.
There's a pitcher of iced tea out there. And I'll go track
down Stan. He's probably at the pool." Meg stopped.
"Unless you'd like to take a dip yourself. I could dig up
a suit for you."

Alexandra, a woman rarely at a loss for words, could
manage no more than a shake of the head. That Greg
had not only gone running back to his old girlfriend,
Meg, at the first opportunity, but that he'd even

brought her down to his father's to witness a heated family squabble, left her speechless. And very depressed.

"You will be staying for dinner, won't you?" Meg said chattily, leading the way to the garden room. If she was bothered by Alexandra's arrival on the scene, she certainly gave no hint of it.

"I'm not sure," Alexandra muttered. What she really wanted to do at that moment was turn and bolt. She wasn't sure why she didn't.

The garden room was shady and cool, its three glassed walls overlooking a beautiful, carefully manicured English garden. The glamorous Meg poured Cassie a tall, frosty glass of iced tea and then glided gracefully off in search of Stanford Hollis.

Without drinking, Alexandra set the glass down and stood staring blindly out at the garden for several minutes.

"Cassie?"

She jumped at the sound of Greg's voice and whirled around. "I . . . didn't hear you come in." She felt suddenly giddy, light-headed.

He glanced down at his feet. "Sneakers." He folded his arms across his broad chest. "But I always seem to be sneaking up on you, don't I?"

Alexandra smiled tentatively. She wished she could get some kind of reading of Greg's mood, but his expression was cool, detached, unreadable.

"You do have a way of surprising me," she said in a low voice, thinking of the exquisite Meg Lincoln.

He smiled wryly. "Well, now we're even. Your showing up here is certainly a big surprise to me. Last I remember, you were on your way to Japan."

Alexandra tried to force her flagging smile back into place. She was terribly dismayed by Greg's manner. She preferred his rage to this studied indifference. "I put Japan on hold."

"Oh? Until when?"

"I'm not sure. A week. Maybe a few weeks." Alexandra tried to keep her voice composed. It was very difficult when she had to pretend not to notice that Greg kept dropping an insolent gaze to her breasts.

Alexandra knew he could feel her discomfort just as she knew he found it comforting. She watched him stroll over to the glass-and-wrought-iron drink cart and pour himself a Scotch on the rocks. "Are you drinking that iced tea, or would you prefer something stronger?" he asked.

"Stronger." The word rasped from her throat.

"What will it be?"

Alexandra shrugged. She rarely drank anything stronger than wine.

He poured a second Scotch on ice and brought it over to her. When she reached for it, their hands touched briefly. Alexandra felt a little volt of current shoot right up her arm. If Greg felt it, he showed no hint.

She fixed her gaze on his face. "I came back to say I'm sorry. No—" she took a swallow of drink, shivering as the burning sensation attacked the back of her throat "—that's not true. I came back because . . ." She took another swallow, this one going down only a fraction easier. "I guess it doesn't matter now. You've found...someone to help you through the rough times."

He looked puzzled, but then he shrugged. "I want to tell you something, Cassie. When I stormed out of your apartment this morning, I vowed to stop trying to figure you out. Nothing that's happened between us makes any sense. Half the things you say, half the things you do, don't make any sense. I thought we had something." He took a swallow of his drink to wet his dry throat, then moved a step closer to her. "But I guess I was wrong."

Alexandra stiffened. "Well, I guess I was wrong about you. You certainly didn't waste much time returning to the fold."

Greg laughed harshly. "You can't mean my father. I doubt he'd see it that way. I just spent a good hour giving him hell for destroying my career. But Stanford can take it. He's tough. Oh, he's tougher than nails. And he's so sure he knows what's best for me that I might have been charging into a brick wall, for all it matters. But—" he leaned ominously closer to her so that Alex picked up the scent of the Scotch "—I'm not about to give up any more than the old man is. No, I'm just going to change my game plan. He likes to play dirty. I can play the same way. After all, he spent so many years and so much money training me that he should be tickled pink it's finally going to pay off."

Alexandra was only half paying attention to Greg's tirade, having caught sight of the striking blonde coming up the path. "I wasn't talking about your father," Alexandra said icily. "I was referring to Meg Lincoln."

For a reason Alexandra couldn't begin to fathom, Greg laughed even harder.

"I don't find anything amusing about what I said," Alexandra responded, seething now. "Miss Lincoln said she was practically one of the family."

"Oh, she is." He smirked.

"She is what?" Meg inquired as she entered through the screen door at one side of the room.

Greg turned around, observing Meg clinically. "Almost one of the family, right, Meg? Let's see," he said, pausing to finish his drink, "when is the wedding date again?"

Meg eyed him petulantly. "My, you have a short memory, Greg. Labor Day, remember?"

Alexandra stared at Greg, stunned. "Married? Labor Day?" No, it was impossible. Greg didn't love Meg. He'd never loved her. Would he really go to such desperate lengths? Had she really hurt him that much? *Oh, Greg, Greg, how could I have messed your life up so thoroughly?*

Alexandra was so distracted she didn't notice Stanford Hollis's entrance at first. When she did, she was once again struck by his forceful presence, his manicured good looks. And once again his smile rang false, his eyes reflecting anger, restraint and even, she thought, a tinge of despair.

He greeted her cordially. If he was surprised by her sudden appearance, he gave no hint of it. But then, a man as carefully controlled as Stanford Hollis wouldn't.

"I was just telling Cassie about the wedding," Greg said with a wry smile. Slowly, his smile broadening, he turned to Cassie. "Don't they make a great-looking couple?" He laughed at the look of astonishment on Cassie's face. "They've been dating for less than a month, but I guess some couples know right off if they're meant for each other. And do you know what, Cassie?" he went on smoothly. "They owe their happiness all to me. I introduced them, you see. It was love at first sight." He moved closer to Alexandra, so close his breath ruffled her hair. "That doesn't happen every day, does it, Cassie? No. Moments like that are rare, aren't they? Or don't you know about that . . . I mean, speaking from personal experience?"

"Greg," Stanford said sharply, "you're in a foul mood. I'm sure your lovely friend isn't deserving of your rudeness."

Greg studied Alexandra thoughtfully. "Yes, she is lovely, isn't she?"

Alexandra was certain Greg was more sober than he wanted anyone here to think he was. "That's all right, Mr. Hollis," Cassie said with a faint smile, her eyes not wavering from Greg's. "I feel that Greg has every right to be in a foul mood. He's been given the shaft all around. From you, from his pal Elroy . . . from me."

"I beg your pardon." Stanford managed to look both affronted and embarrassed at the same time.

Alexandra's smile vanished as she looked from Greg's surprised expression to his father's. "A person," she said evenly, "deserves a chance to make his own choice about his life's work. The way I see it, a parent, a friend . . . a lover, ought to be there to offer him support, love, understanding." She hesitated, but only for a moment. "As Greg's father, Mr. Hollis, oughtn't you to be the first to share your son's joys, help ease his disappointments, his pain? Certainly do everything in your power not to cause him more pain? A parent should cherish his child. And above all else, Mr. Hollis, he should never, never betray that child's trust. Or how can he expect love and trust in return?"

When Alexandra stopped, she was trembling, the air was absolutely still and everyone else in the room was mute. And then suddenly Greg began to clap slowly. "Bravo, Cassie. A fine speech."

"Really, Greg, between you and your girlfriend here, your father and I have had quite enough," Meg said sharply.

Greg clapped louder, aiming his applause in Meg's direction. "You're good, too, Meggy. What a proper, stern stepmother you're going to make."

Stanford Hollis was the only one who didn't say his piece. Without a word, without a look at any of them, he turned abruptly and strode out of the room. Meg was quick to follow him.

Alexandra was flushed as she stared across at Greg. "I guess I said more than I had a right to."

His smile was bemused. "You never cease to amaze me. You'd make a great defense attorney." A touch of warmth snaked into his tone. And Alexandra smiled.

But Greg was wary of that smile. He didn't know what to make of her canceling her trip. He told himself he'd be a fool to trust her. He could turn his back any time, and she'd be ducking out again. His wariness showed in his face, and Alexandra despaired. She was pretty sure she could read his mind. And she couldn't very well blame him for being on his guard.

"Hey, don't look so worried, Cassie. You were good. Very gutsy. But just what provoked the sermon?" All hint of tenderness was gone as Greg drew behind his protective shell.

Alexandra flinched. "I spoke to Steve Elroy."

Greg's eyes narrowed. "I see. And what exactly did my old pal Elroy tell you?"

"Well . . . he told me everything." She hesitated, realizing that Elroy had even alluded to Stanford Hollis's involvement with one of Greg's old girlfriends. Now she was able to put two and two together about the remark Greg had made to his father the day before about not acting his age. Obviously, Stanford Hollis felt a need to compete with Greg and control him on all levels, personal and professional. Couldn't the man see what his actions were doing to his relationship with his son? "I think what your father did was contemptible, Greg. I know how much it must hurt...."

His features darkened still more. "Save the sympathy, Cassie. I'm not hurt. I'm angry as hell. And just for the record, I can fight my own battles. And I certainly can handle my father on my own."

"Can you?"

He nodded slowly. "And," he said, his gaze moving over her now, his mouth twisted slightly downward in an expression of mockery, "I can handle you, too."

Alexandra's nostrils flared perceptibly. "Can you, now?"

He rubbed his jaw. "You waltz great, Cassie. Not only on the ballroom floor. You seem very skilled at waltzing in and out of my life. I never seem to know just which direction you're heading."

Alexandra's eyes darted away from him, but he cupped her chin, forcing her full attention on him.

"For a while there," he went on, his voice very cool, "all I seemed to be doing was trying to keep up with some very fancy footwork of yours. You got me out of breath, Cass. I guess I'm just not cut out for following someone as . . . expert as you. So from here on, you're either going to have to find a new partner, or learn to do the dance my way." His mouth curved in a cynical sneer. "Then again, maybe I'll give up dancing altogether for a while."

Placing her hands on her hips, Alexandra shot him an indignant glare. But before she could say anything,

Greg released his hold on her chin and strode abruptly across the room and out the door.

He was halfway up the garden path when Alexandra called after him. "Where are you going?"

"Home," he shouted back, picking up his pace.

Alexandra grabbed her purse and ran up the path, catching up to Greg at his car, a snappy white Triumph, parked by the front of the house. He was just sliding in behind the wheel.

"Give me a lift back," she said, out of breath from running. Then she added, "Please."

He gave a barely perceptible nod, and Alexandra slid in beside him.

Greg was stoically silent as he drove. He looked so formidable Alexandra couldn't find the courage to speak until he turned up Fifth Avenue nearly an hour later. "How do you feel about your father and Meg?" Alexandra asked hesitantly.

He cast her a quick glance, not answering.

"I think Steve Elroy was afraid you'd be upset," she said.

"Why should I feel upset?"

"I...I thought...you and Meg..." she stammered realizing that, as Cassie, she wouldn't know much about his relationship with Meg.

He gave her a curious look. "I noticed that you thought Meg and I were a twosome when we were back at my father's house."

"Well, Meg mentioned to me...that you were...good friends. I got the idea, from the way she said it, that there might have been a time when you were...more than that."

His only answer was a wry smile as he pulled to a stop in front of her building.

"Here we are," he said blithely, hands resting on the steering wheel, engine running, eyes straight ahead.

Alexandra stared at him in frustration. Then swinging the door open, she stepped out, muttering, "You *are* a difficult man, Greg Hollis. A very difficult man."

THREE DAYS PASSED. Alexandra waited for Greg to call, but she wasn't surprised when he didn't make any effort to contact her. Over and over she told herself to leave bad enough alone and just get on the next plane to San Francisco. But somehow she couldn't leave. Not until she knew what was really ticking in Greg's mind. To find that out, she figured she'd have to wait for one of his letters. He might play his feelings close to his chest from now on with Cassie, but he'd confide in Alexandra. Surely he'd write her soon. He always did when he was in a crisis. But no letters came.

Finally Alexandra couldn't stand it any longer and got up her courage to call him. The first time she tried, his answering service said he was unavailable. So she waited until the evening, phoning him a second time a little after nine.

Greg picked up the phone on the fifth ring. "Yeah, hello." His voice sounded rough, as if she'd awakened him.

"Greg, it's Cassie. I just wanted to find out how you were doing."

"I'm doing just—" He stopped, breaking into a fit of coughing. "Fine," he finished huskily.

"You don't sound fine."

He started to answer, but he had another coughing attack.

"Greg, you're sick."

"A brilliant deduction, Watson."

"It's your throat, isn't it? It's all my fault."

"Forget it."

"I can't, Greg. I can't."

He sighed heavily. "Try, Cassie. For my sake."

The next moment Alexandra was holding a dead line. It slowly sank in that Greg had simply hung up on her. For more than thirty seconds Alexandra sat there in a daze staring at the phone, then anger swelled inside her. "Okay, Mr. Hollis," she muttered indignantly, "if that's the way you want to end it, it's just fine with me. Fine? It's more than fine. It's perfect. I couldn't have arranged it better myself. I'm just glad I got to see what you're really like. And I was fool enough to think you were so special, so different. Why, you're no different at all."

11

IN THE ELEVATOR a little while later she considered what she would say to Greg. Tell him off for hanging up on her? No. She couldn't really blame him. She couldn't blame him for his anger, his pain, his confusion. Why was she here? What did she want from Greg? What could she hope to gain? So many questions. But she had no answers. She only knew he was now physically, as well as emotionally, drained. And in so many ways she was responsible on all counts.

Her legs felt rubbery as she exited the elevator on the eleventh floor. Greg had buzzed her into the building, but only after a long, considered pause.

He was waiting by the door, wearing a blue cotton robe, looking scruffy, exhausted, watery-eyed . . . and very, very guarded.

"Why'd you come?" His voice was raspy and querulous.

It wasn't a question she could easily answer. Instead of trying, she sidestepped it. "You look awful."

"Just a cold," he muttered, making no move to invite her in.

Alexandra smiled. "Right. Just a cold." She hesitated. "I think I know how you must be feeling."

Was that a brief flicker of tenderness in his hazel eyes? It was so fleeting Alexandra couldn't be sure.

"You ought to be in bed."

A twisted smile tugged at the corners of his mouth. "Is that why you came over?"

"I doubt either one of us has the strength at the moment to make love or do battle." She brushed by him and stepped into his apartment.

"Did I invite you in?"

Alexandra grinned. "You're not the only one, Greg Hollis, who shows up uninvited. Now direct me to the kitchen. You go back to bed."

"TAKE IT." Alexandra held out the aspirin tablet.

"Go away," Greg growled, pulling the covers over his head.

"Stop behaving like a child."

"Stop behaving like my mother."

"And you told *me* I was a lousy patient."

"You were."

"Well, you're no great shakes, Mr. Hollis."

"I didn't ask you to come over here and take care of me, did I?"

Alexandra arched a brow. "I don't recall having asked you to nurse me, either. Let's just say I'm giving you a taste of your own medicine."

He let the covers fall from his face. "Give me the damn pill."

Alexandra smiled sweetly, handing it over with a glass of water.

"Okay, now leave me alone," he said, swallowing it with a grimace.

Alexandra's smile widened. "I guess I should be thankful you haven't taken a swing at me."

Greg's eyes narrowed. "Don't think the thought hasn't occurred to me."

"YOU LOOK EXHAUSTED," Greg said groggily when Alexandra stepped into his room the next morning with a breakfast tray bearing weak tea and a three-minute egg.

"Thanks." She grinned. "You look rested, though. How do you feel?"

"Not too bad. I guess," he said with a hint of drawl in his voice, "I mend quickly."

She felt herself stiffen as she brought the tray over. "Sit up."

"Were you here all night?"

"Yes. What if you'd had a bad dream?"

Greg was about to come back with a snappy remark, but instead he leaned on his elbows, studying her thoughtfully. "I keep telling myself not to be surprised by anything you do, Cassie Phillips." His eyes trailed her face. "Why'd you come over last night? I thought after our phone conversation . . ."

"I was furious at you for hanging up on me. But I was also worried about you. You sounded so sick. I guess my worry won out." She started to set the breakfast tray on the bed.

"Why don't we eat together in the dining room? Just give me a couple of minutes to shower."

Alexandra hesitated.

"Were you about to ask if I needed any help?" he said.

She flushed. "No. Of course not." She turned away, tray in hand. "I'll do another egg for you when you're finished."

She went back to the kitchen and threw the egg out and poured the tea back into the pot. Then she went into Greg's dining room, which was actually an L off the living room. She began clearing papers from the lovely oak table, thinking to herself how often over the years she'd wondered about the place Greg lived. She liked his apartment, liked how much it seemed to suit him. It was large, airy, masculine and yet warm, with its soft beige walls, toffee-colored carpeting, a thoughtful blend of antique and modern furnishings, the upholstered pieces in earth-tone tweeds.

An envelope slipped from the pile of papers in her arms. She bent to pick it up, pausing as she saw the handwriting. It was one of hers. There was her name and address in neat, tidy script in the upper left-hand corner of the envelope. She felt the oddest chill. It turned quickly to heat as she heard Greg come up behind her.

"I . . . I was just clearing off the table," she said, hurriedly rising and dumping the whole pile of papers on the buffet against the wall. "I'll get the food," she said rushing into the kitchen where she had a most untimely attack of hiccups. She was gulping down a glass of water when Greg's hand reached out from behind her, turning off the faucet.

"What's the matter?" His gaze was narrowed on her flushed face.

She spun around. "Nothing." It didn't make matters easier for Alexandra that all Greg was wearing at the moment was a pair of tight-fitting jeans that he'd not even bothered to snap at the waist.

"I thought you might be wondering about that letter. Wondering," he said, one corner of his mouth quirking, "who Alexandra Yates is."

Her breath caught, suspended in her lungs. "It's . . . none of my business."

She saw the corners of his eyes crinkle, a hint of amusement creeping in, and she grew more flushed.

"She's a friend. A very good friend. You might say we've endured the test of time. When all else crumbles around me, I can always depend on Alex. Her best quality is that she never pulls any punches. She's always been straight with me. And I've always been straight with her."

Alexandra's mind was like a forest of frightened animals all scurrying about for safety from an oncoming storm. Did Greg suspect? Was he playing with her? Or merely trying to provoke her jealousy? Whatever his intent, he was making her crazy.

She started to move away from the sink only to find herself imprisoned by Greg's arms, his hands gripping the counter edge. "You wouldn't know about playing it straight with someone, though, would you, Cassie?"

His voice was husky with a blend of hurt and desire. His hair was damp and tousled. His hazel eyes were luminous. Alexandra thought her heart would break as she looked at him. The memory of their lovemaking crept unbidden into her mind as she tried to keep from looking at his naked torso. Half of her wished she'd never come here last night; half of her wished he'd pull her into his arms this instant, make her feel whole again, alive.

Instead, he made no move at all, either to embrace her or release her.

"Breakfast. We . . . should eat." Even she could hear the desperation in her voice. Her breathing was erratic, and she could feel Greg's gaze fixed on her face, but she was transfixed by his broad chest.

"Are you hungry, Cassie?" His voice slid over her like silk.

Her breath caught in her throat, and a sharp thrill jolted like lightning through her body. Yes. Oh yes, she was hungry. Desperately hungry with an ache that would not listen to reason.

"Tell me, Cassie. Tell me what you want. Be straight with me—just this once."

A dramatic tension filled the air. She knew she was doomed to heartbreak whether she lied or told the truth. Just this once . . . She drew a deep, sharp breath. "You," she whispered, a rush of recklessness sweeping over her. "I want you, Greg. Oh, I want you so very much."

He slid his right hand around her shoulders, pulling her against him, his mouth finding hers in a hard, urgent kiss, his fingers descending into her thick, wild hair.

She kissed him back passionately. She could feel his heat permeate her thin cotton blouse. The heat sank into her skin. It felt so good, so incredibly good, to be in his arms, to be engulfed by him.

She moaned a little as he unbuttoned her blouse, sliding it off her shoulders. Then her bra. Her high, firm breasts pressed against his naked chest, her nipples already hard. His hands slid down to her narrow waist. Her arms moved around his neck as he devoured her parted lips.

The kiss was intense but all too brief. Alexandra felt the gentle but firm pressure of Greg's hands as he forced her back. She gasped at the separation. She could feel her entire body beating to the rhythm of her pulse. Even apart, his heat was transmitted to her. The intangible force of his desire enveloped her.

The apartment was so still that the sound of their mingled breaths was magnified. Greg's gaze fell to her breasts. She was incredible, he thought. Her body seemed to glow with an inner light. From the first, he knew the impossibility of keeping his hands off her.

"Cassie," he said softly, leaning down to kiss her tenderly.

She wanted to feel the pressure once again of his body pressed to hers, but he restrained her as she attempted to arch against him.

"Greg . . ." She whispered his name with longing and frustration.

"Not yet, Cassie." His hazel eyes bore into her. "Did you know this was going to happen? Did you want it to happen? Is that why you didn't leave for Japan? Is that why you came here?"

He held her by the shoulders now.

"Too many questions. I . . . I don't know any of the answers, Greg. I can't think straight. All I know is that . . . I can't fight this . . . need."

"Cassie, talk to me. Tell me why this is so incredibly hard for you." He stared into her frightened eyes. "Will it help if I tell you?"

"How can you?"

"You love me, Cassie. You've been fighting it so hard that it's nearly driven you crazy." A rueful smile crossed his lips. "And me." He took a deep breath. "Loving me terrifies you."

"Yes." The admission escaped her lips. And then very quickly, "No. No, I'm not in love. I'm not ready for love. I can't . . . I have to leave . . . for Japan . . . soon. And . . . I'll be there for a long time. I've got to do this. I have no choice. Everything . . . depends on it." Her face wrenched in pain. "We have no future, Greg. You must understand that. We must both accept that."

She tried again to escape, but his grip on her shoulders tightened. He shook her so that her hair flew across her face. Her lips trembled.

"I love you, Cassie."

"No. No, Greg. Don't say it."

"Is it so awful?"

"Why won't you understand?" Her voice was almost a sob.

"Okay, okay. You're dedicated to your career. In a short time you leave for Japan. Maybe, just maybe, we'll never see each other again." He smiled. "Then again, maybe you'll go to Japan only to discover you can't live without me after all," he said deliberately. "At least give me a chance to make that a possibility, Cassie. Give me a chance to make it hard for you to forget me."

"It's already hard," she said miserably. "But in the end I will still go, Greg. There I'm being straight with you. I will leave. I must." Her voice took on a pleading edge.

He nodded slowly. "When is the latest you can leave?"

She hesitated. *Get out fast*, she told herself, *before things blow up in your face.* But in the end, as she looked into Greg's warm, loving, passion-filled eyes, she whispered, "The end of August . . . at the very latest."

He smiled. "Good." His smile broadened. "I'm still hungry. How about you?"

Her own smile was tremulous. "Ravenous."

"Let's go into the bedroom."

THEIR ARMS PULLED them to each other, face to face, flesh to flesh. His hands gripped her taut hips, pressing her closer. Greg's face was rough against her cheek, his texture thrillingly familiar.

"From the first moment I saw you, I knew," he whispered, finding her lips, his hands moving in gentle, caressing circles down her spine.

As Alexandra shared the kiss fully, the outer world shrank away. The time for guilt, remorse, doubts, was gone. There was only this searing need. *Yes, my darling, from the first moment . . .*

"Oh, Greg," she whispered, all of her emotions—joy, sorrow, passion—mirrored in the haunted longing of her voice. Her hand slid down between their bodies, taking him in her hand, encircling him, caressing him, her strokes moving in concert with his breathing.

The faintest strand of a blues tune from a neighboring apartment mingled with their shallow breaths as they tumbled mutely on Greg's double bed.

She loved the feel of his firm, lean body. She loved the strong, tangy scent of him. She loved the way his kisses seared right through her. She loved the high-voltage excitement that streaked through both of them, connecting them, making them one. She loved him. And making love with him was the one way she could express that love openly, uninhibitedly. This time it was even better than the other times for Alexandra. She had, in a certain way, told him the truth, given herself the freedom of more time. And she intended to make the most of it.

Greg lovingly explored each part of her body, a wild sweetness coursing through him at the satin-smooth warmth of her. His tongue slid in a delicious line down her throat. "I love the way you taste," he whispered. His tongue trailed lower. He felt the tensing of her muscles as he captured a taut nipple, sucking it deep into his mouth. She pressed tight against him, straining. Her hands pulled his head up, hungry for his kisses.

She murmured his name, unashamedly twining her legs around him, her hands stroking down his back and buttocks now. He heard her gasp with pleasure as he entered her, raising his head from her breast as she shuddered with each deep, penetrating thrust.

He braced his weight on his forearms as Alexandra arched beneath him, the pressure of her hands on his buttocks drawing him deep inside her again and again.

His hands cupped her head, his fingers spreading wide over her hair. Her legs were hooked around his knees. He thrilled to her whispered endearments, her murmured words of pleasure, her eager lips, her writhing hips as he moved against her, the ecstatic look in her eyes as their gazes met and held.

Greg could feel the pressure building in him. Alexandra sensed his trying to hold back. "It's all right, darling," she whispered, her supple body arching harder into him with each stroke, until he exploded inside her, a flood tide of sensations shuddering every muscle in his body.

Alexandra kept stroking him, caressing him, kissing him. She smoothed back his damp hair. They rolled over, their bodies still connected, still full of electric energy. She felt him filling the center of her being, her ecstasy continuing to climb as his silken intimate stroking began once more.

He marveled at how quickly he grew aroused again, his mind and body propelled once more into that galaxy of pure pleasure. She smiled down at him, her face dazzling, driving a liquid heat through his entire body.

Her yearning soared. Words were no longer possible as desire filled her; only crooning sounds emanated from her, sounds filled with lust and love, passion fiercely entwined with the emotional bond that made it all so right, so incredibly sweet.

Greg fought to catch his breath, his exhalations almost fiery.

"Ohhh . . ." exploded from her throat as her whole body quivered, her pleasure throwing her free of time and rootedness until she was rushing with the wind, Greg soaring with her in the space of a heartbeat, linked by the bond of pleasure and love.

"How long have you been a fashion designer?"

They were sitting in bed finishing a late breakfast. Alexandra's hand trembled as she held her cup, a few droplets of tea spilling onto the sheet. "Five years or so."

"Is that what you always wanted to do?"

"When I was seven," she said, "I wanted to be a ballerina."

He smiled. "When I was a kid, I wanted to be a magician."

Yes, Alexandra said silently, *I know.* He'd written her about his childhood dreams, his fantasies.

"What did your father think of that?" she asked.

"I suppose he wouldn't have minded so much if he'd thought I was good at it. But I was awful. Not that it mattered to me. And my mother . . ." He hesitated. "She always told me I could do anything I set my mind to do."

"My mother always told me to be practical, sensible, cautious. She worried a lot." Alexandra grinned. "I certainly have thrown her caution to the winds, haven't I?"

"Are you sorry?"

"No. I've never felt happier."

"Even when you're designing?"

Alexandra flushed. "It's different."

"Yes. I know."

Her own discomfort vanished at the sound of the sadness in his voice.

"What will you do now that the Gilrand project has folded?"

Greg didn't answer right away. "I haven't decided what to do."

Alexandra set her cup on the bedside table. "What did you mean about playing dirty, like your father?"

Greg turned to her. "I don't suppose I will now." He smiled. "I'm very glad you didn't run off as planned, Cassie. Being with you puts things into perspective. I was so angry."

"And hurt?" *Tell me, Greg. Tell me the truth. Don't save it all for letters. Don't play it so safe.*

A bittersweet smile played on his lips. "Yes," he said in a low, husky voice. "And hurt."

She touched his cheek. He captured her hand, brought it to his lips, kissing the soft, silky skin of her palm.

"I may get the Gilrand project back," he said, pressing her hand against his chest so that she could feel his heartbeat.

"What do you mean?"

"There's a flaw in the design Elroy gave my father. I was going to wait until the deal had been signed and sealed to let the old man know, then let him come crawling to me, having to beg me to solve the problem. I'm not bragging, but he knows as well as I do that I'm the only one who could do it. Elroy knows it, too. I was angry—and hurt enough—to want to have the pleasure of telling them all exactly what they could do with that design."

"And now?"

He drew her to him. "Now I have other pleasures to be grateful for. I don't need revenge." He smoothed her hair. "I need you." He kissed her lightly but tenderly on the lips. "I'll play it straight with dear old Dad before he walks into a very large loss. Then it's up to him. Maybe Elroy or someone else will come up with a new design. Or maybe New Amsterdam Life will decide to find a less inconvenient spot to stick a new building. I guess I'll just have to wait and see how vindictive my father cares to be." A hardness crept into his voice, his arms tightening around her so that she gasped.

"Sorry," he said, loosening his hold. "My father and I have been engaged in a cold war for a long time. I guess this is going to bring it to a head. Either he'll declare all-out war, or else he'll have to enter negotiations for a peace treaty. Knowing my father, he's never been very good at negotiating anything with me."

"Oh, Greg," Alexandra said softly, "I can't believe he doesn't want peace as much as you do."

He smiled ruefully. "You'd have to know our history to understand where I'm coming from, Cass." He tightened his hold again, but this time his grip was rough with desire, not anger. "I don't want to talk about history now, babe. I want to make some of our own."

Alexandra smiled as his mouth captured hers. Once more their bodies were stirred, and she gave herself up to the delicious thrill of making love again.

New York
August 20

Dear Alex,
I'm not knocking your words of caution, but I'm

not afraid of taking a risk this time. Okay, Cassie
still insists she'll leave at the end of August, which
means two more weeks. But a lot can happen in
two weeks. She's in love with me, Alex. It's plain
from her every look, her every word. For all her
talk about her fierce devotion to her work, I
haven't seen her so much as pick up a pencil to
sketch an apron since we've been together. That
can only mean one of two things: she's lost her
touch, or I've managed to drive all thoughts of
work from her mind. You know which one I'll bet
on.

And talking of work, my father's still out of
town on business, putting everything on hold. I
have a feeling he's scouring the country for another architect to come up with a workable rendering. But given the amount of square footage
New Amsterdam Life needs, I doubt he'll find
anyone but me to figure out a design that will be
possible on the Gilrand land. At least he knows
better than to push me on the matter. Thanks to
Cassie's outburst down at his place, I actually believe the old man is feeling his first twinges of guilt.
I know your advice is to have it all out with him.
Even Cassie's been at me to try to talk to the old
man. I guess I'm just not ready. Right now I have
more important things on my mind.

You'd be proud of me, Alex. I've played it cool
with Cassie. No commitments, no obligations, no
pursuit. I've given her all the leeway she could ever
ask for. And it's working like a charm. She's become more open, responsive, eager... Well, you
can read between the lines.

Anyway, it's all part of my secret plan to make her see that she can't live without me. I've got all the details worked out. Just before she takes off for Japan, I'm going to ask her to marry me. When she protests that she's got to leave, that she has no idea how long she'll be gone, I'll whip out my plane ticket to Japan along with a shiny gold wedding band. Why not go with her? Even if the Gilrand project falls into my lap again, I'm pretty sure I can put it on hold for a few months. There's nothing to stop me, Alex. And I have a gut feeling Cassie won't be able to refuse me.

So, Alex, while I'm working toward my happy ending, how about working toward one of your own? Wouldn't it be fantastic, Alex, if we both found that route to a happily-ever-after finale?

Love as always,
Greg

Alexandra crumpled the letter in her trembling hands, stinging tears blurring her eyes. These love-filled weeks with Greg had not been eternal. They had only felt that way for her. For a short while she'd fooled herself into living as if summer were the only season there was. She had had love, passion, laughter, joy. But it was all about to end. The summer was being swallowed up, Greg's letter wrenching it from her before she was ready to relinquish it. She could do nothing about that.

He'd tricked her—her as Cassie—into believing that the parting would go smoothly. He'd been warm, loving, wonderfully understanding, undemanding. He'd lulled her into thinking they could have this moment in time and then graciously let it slip into memory. Her own thoughts had been so full of him that she'd pushed aside all thoughts of how hard separation would be for her, how bittersweet the memories would be, how all summers from here on out would serve to remind her of what she had captured and lost.

She rose from the couch. Nothing would be resolved by allowing herself to wallow in misery. As she walked over to the telephone, she told herself that she'd had nearly two months of incredible happiness. It was, she told herself as she dialed, quite a lot.

"Could I please make a reservation for the next flight to San Francisco?"

She gripped the receiver tightly while she was put on hold. "Yes," she said resolutely after a minute's wait. "Seven o'clock tonight will be fine." Again a pause, hot tears taunting the corners of her eyes. "No. That will be one way only.'

IT WASN'T that Greg was untroubled or even all that sure of himself. There was still, even after all these weeks, so much about Cassie that was a mystery to him. For a woman who proclaimed such a devotion to her career, she never even spoke of it to him. But he'd done a bit of snooping, contacting a couple of models he knew. According to them, Cassie Phillips was, indeed, one of the rising stars in the fashion industry. One of the models even knew about her designs being sold in boutiques in Japan.

As for her history, her past life, Cassie gave very little away. Oh, she answered his questions, but she never volunteered anything. And there were times when he could see a flash of pain in her eyes when he asked her about the man she'd once loved, the man that he had reminded her of at first.

But for all his puzzlement, he knew one thing for certain. She loved him as much as he loved her. Love, he told himself, perhaps naively, would conquer all problems. Love would eventually soothe all doubts and fears. Love would slowly erode the barriers they had both erected to keep from getting hurt again.

He was thinking just these wonderfully optimistic thoughts when he stepped into the drugstore at the corner of Cassie's street to pick up an evening edition of the newspaper on the way to her apartment.

It was her name in bold black lettering on the left-hand corner of a fashion magazine that caught Greg's eye immediately. Then he took in the whole heading. Fashion Designer Cassie Phillips Shapes Bold New Trends in Japan.

"WHERE IS SHE?"

The doorman stepped back warily as Greg's voice boomed. "She left, sir."

"When?"

"A little over an hour ago."

"Where'd she go?"

"I really don't know. I only know she isn't planning to come back. She returned her keys. And I heard her tell the cabdriver to take her to Kennedy."

Greg tore at the pages of the magazine he'd purchased instead of the newspaper until he came to the page he was looking for. He held it up. It showed not only some brightly colored evening dresses but a photo of the couturier in the upper left-hand corner. "This is Cassie Phillips, isn't it?"

The doorman wiped his wet brow, shrugging. "I suppose so, sir," he muttered, reading the caption under the picture.

"And the other woman?"

"The other woman?"

Greg grabbed the poor frightened man by the collar.

"She's . . . she's been staying at . . . Miss Phillips's apartment," the doorman stammered.

"I know that much," Greg snarled. "Who is she? What's her name?"

"I...I don't know. I just started here a few weeks ago. I'm just temporary until they put in a new intercom system."

The ashen-faced man looked relieved when Greg released his hold. But the fierce expression on Greg's face continued to make him very nervous.

Greg's gaze shifted to the magazine article. Then without warning he threw the magazine to the ground, gave the doorman a scornful glance and strode toward the revolving doors.

When he got there, he suddenly came to an abrupt halt, whirled around and headed back again. The doorman began to shake in earnest.

"Sorry," Greg muttered. "I didn't mean to take my frustration out on you." He picked up the magazine and left.

Once outside, Greg took in gulps of air, trying to steady his nerves. Then he went around the corner to a dimly lit bar, took a seat at a table in the far corner near a window and flipped open the magazine again to the page featuring the photo of Cassie Phillips, alias Karen.

He stared at the photo for a long time, not touching the Scotch he'd ordered. Traffic roared and screeched outside, the setting sun casting dark shadows over the bustling thoroughfare. Greg was oblivious to the sights and sounds. Numb with the pain of betrayal, he finally rose, threw some money onto the table and left, walking through the night-shrouded streets of the city back to his apartment across town.

12

Dear Greg,

I feel your pain as if it were my own. I wish I could find the words to comfort you. But I know how little words mean when you're engulfed by pain. Maybe the only answer is to struggle through the hurt. Greg, you had something wonderful for a brief time. You discovered feelings and needs you never knew existed. Did she only give you pain, Greg? Did she? I don't believe that. I believe she gave you her love, but that something beyond even her impelled her to flee.

Yes, she deceived you. Yes, she lied about who she was, what she did. I can't tell you why she did that any more than you can. Perhaps she was in some terrible trouble, her real identity putting her at great risk. Obviously the real Cassie Phillips thinks so. That must be why she hasn't responded to your wires or your long-distance calls to Japan.

I only pray that you don't let the hurt make you bitter. I hope in time you will take new risks, find new joy. I truly want that for you, Greg. I want you to be happy.

Okay, hate her if you must. What she did was cruel, even if it might have been unintentional.

Hate her, Greg. Not yourself. You're not a fool.
You just fell in love. And when people fall in love,
they can do the most inexplicable things. My heart
is with you.

All my love,
Alex

"EXCUSE ME, but would you like the chipped beef or the
fried chicken?" the flight attendant asked.

Greg looked up and smiled distractedly at the pretty
blonde. Folding Alexandra's letter, he tucked it into the
breast pocket of his shirt. "Just bring me a Scotch and
soda."

"You don't want anything to eat?"

He tapped his flat, muscular stomach. "A touch of
indigestion."

The attractive flight attendant leaned toward him.
"Would you like me to see if I could find something to
make you feel better?" Her voice was languid, her smile
curling around him in a conspiratorial caress.

Greg merely shrugged. Being the object of pursuit
had lost its glow. "No, thanks. How long till we land in
San Francisco?"

"Another couple of hours." She paused. "Ever been
there before?"

"A couple of times."

"It's a beautiful city. My very favorite. I know some
wonderful 'in' places." She arched a well-plucked brow.

Greg smiled. "I'm visiting a very close friend who
lives there."

"A lady friend."

Greg nodded.

"Lucky lady." The attendant straightened, gave Greg a perfunctory wave and moved up the aisle to the next row of seats.

Greg leaned back and shut his eyes, wincing. He hadn't lied about the indigestion, but he knew its cause was strictly emotional. He was about to break a special pact. He wasn't even sure why. A need to connect with the one woman who had been the only person to remain loyal and true to him all these years? A self-destructive wish to ruin the one sure thing in his life? Mounting concern because, since that letter he'd gotten from Alexandra nearly three weeks ago, he hadn't received so much as a postcard from her? Perhaps it was all those things. And something more. He felt utterly at loose ends. And he had this gut feeling that only Alex could help him tie them together.

"ALEX, YOU CAN'T go on torturing yourself. It's pointless," Jill pleaded as she watched her roommate tear up another sheet of mauve stationery.

"I can't write him. I keep trying, but I can't." Alexandra tossed the paper toward the trash basket, missing it by a few feet but tagging Nell. The dog yelped, gave Alexandra a hurt glance and crawled under the bed.

"See, even Nell can't stand it anymore," Jill said, giving Alexandra a glance remarkably similar to the dog's.

Alexandra managed a weak smile. "I'm sorry, Jill. I know I've been impossible to live with this last month. I keep thinking I'm going to be able to pull myself together. I really do a decent job of it when I'm at work. But once I get home . . ."

"You have to start going out again, Alex. Even to get together with friends for a movie or drinks. But you turn us all down."

"I'd just be a drag."

"Alex, you showed me that last letter you wrote Greg. Shouldn't you follow the same advice you gave him? You have to put what happened into perspective. You have to get on with your life." Jill stopped abruptly, a wry smile curving her lips. "Would you just listen to me? I sound like one of those self-help, pop-psychology books. What am I saying? God, Alex, I'm sorry. You want to feel miserable, then go ahead. Feel miserable. I'd feel pretty miserable myself if I had to give up the man of my dreams. I'd feel downright miserable."

Tears spiked Alexandra's eyes, but this time her smile wasn't forced. She rose and put her arms around her roommate. "Thanks, Jill," she whispered. "You're a good friend."

GREG CHECKED into the Fairmont, calling down to room service for dinner, most of which he ended up leaving untouched. Being here in San Francisco, knowing that the next day he'd see Alexandra Yates for the first time, gave him a first-class case of nerves. Meeting her face-to-face and somehow trying to explain why he'd come when he himself wasn't all that sure why was going to be a tough trick to pull off. What if she was furious at him for breaking their sacred pact? What if she told him he'd blown it and it was all over? No more letters. No more Alexandra. Could he bear yet another excruciating loss?

Sometime in the midst of tossing and turning in bed in the middle of the night, he decided on a plan of action that finally allowed him to drift off to sleep.

Staring at himself in the bathroom mirror the next morning he told himself that he could still change his mind and catch the first flight back to New York. No one would be any the wiser. But he knew he wouldn't do that. The need to see her had grown into a compulsion. He no longer tried to fathom why. Carefully rethinking his plan of action, he gave his reflection a reassuring nod.

A HALF HOUR LATER Greg was standing in the shadow of the school building where Alexandra worked, squinting, mouth dry, heart pounding. Just two minutes ago he'd gotten his first look at Alexandra Yates.

The crazy thing was he wasn't all that surprised by what he'd seen. Now if someone had walked up to him just a minute before that fateful peek and said, "Hey, man, I'll tell you the real identity of the woman who went around calling herself Cassie Phillips. She's none other than your nine-year-long penpal and confidante, Alexandra Yates," Greg would have told that person he was out of his mind. For one thing, the whole time he'd been with Cassie, Alex had been writing him from San Francisco. For another, Alex, of all people on earth, wouldn't betray him.

So why, when he'd sneaked that look through the glass-paneled door of Alexandra Yates's office, did the surprise of seeing the woman he'd known as Cassie Phillips not throw him for a bigger loop?

Because in that instant it all made sense. All the pieces fit. The jigsaw puzzle was complete. And looking back, he even realized a part of him had sensed it nearly from the beginning. Her warmth, her sensitivity, her intuitive understanding, her apprehension and elusiveness . . . her hiccups.

He caught a cab, grateful for one thing. Alexandra hadn't spotted him. A cynical sneer slashed his lips as he revised his plan.

JILL HUNG UP the telephone and walked into her roommate's bedroom. Alexandra was curled up on the bed.

She'd been half dozing, but when Jill walked in, Alexandra's eyes opened abruptly. "What is it?" she asked, disturbed by the look of consternation on Jill's face.

"That was Greg on the telephone."

"Greg? My Greg? Calling me? He's never called me. What did he say?" Alexandra was sitting up stiffly in the bed now.

Jill hesitated. "He's here, Alex."

"Here? Here in San Francisco?"

Jill grimaced. "Here on Polk Street."

"Our Polk Street," Alexandra squealed, shaking her head. "But he . . . he can't be!"

"He is."

Alexandra leaped from the bed, scurrying around the room like a mad woman. "Oh my God, I've got to get out of here. I've got—"

"Alex, he's on his way up. Right now. If you go dashing out that front door, you're going to run smack dab into him."

Alexandra looked at Jill in panic. Panic turned to despair. Then a moment later an idea struck. "Wait. Wait a second. He doesn't have the faintest idea what I look like. Even what I sound like." She was looking at Jill intently now.

Jill backed up. "Hold on, Alex. I don't like the wheels I hear spinning in that devious mind of yours."

"Jill, you have to help me. You're my friend. You can't let me down now. There's no other solution."

"Alex—"

Alexandra gripped Jill's arm. "Please, Jill. Listen, it will be easy. Just pretend you're me, see him for a minute, tell him you... you have to go out. Tell him he shouldn't have come. Tell him he was wrong to break the pact we'd made. I mean, the pact you two had made. Oh, Jill—"

The shrill sound of the front doorbell silenced Alexandra abruptly. "Please," she mouthed once more to Jill.

After a moment Jill shrugged. "Okay, okay. But I'm telling you right now, Alex, I don't think I'm going to be able to pull it off."

As Jill started out of the bedroom, Alexandra caught hold of her once more. "Thanks...Alex," she said with a whisper of a smile.

GREG GLANCED IDLY around the living room, a small but artfully decorated space. The far wall housed bookshelves and a stereo, the near wall was exposed brick and displayed colorful prints attractively framed. The furnishings were simple but tasteful, a deep blue corduroy couch, a couple of comfortable, patterned armchairs and a low, marble coffee table covered with an eclectic mix of magazines.

"You've really caught me completely off guard, Greg," Jill said, her heart beating overtime. Why had she ever let Alex talk her into this charade? It was going terribly. Greg had insisted on coming in, and despite her telling him she had a date, he showed no sign of leaving.

He sat down on the corduroy couch and looked up at her. "I had to see you, Alex. I'm falling apart, and I had no one else I could turn to."

"But . . . we had a pact."

He smiled, a hint of seduction slipping out. "We have more than that. I need you, Alex." He patted the cushion beside him.

"Come and sit down next to me. Talk to me, Alex. You can't desert me. You, of all people, can't walk out on me. You're not Cassie. You have integrity. You really care." He was up, walking toward her.

Before Jill knew what was happening, he was pulling her into his arms. "Please, Alex. I need comforting so badly. You're the only one, Alex. You're the only one who can help me to forget."

Jill had to admit one thing. Greg Hollis was certainly an attractive man. And a persistent one. *Alex doesn't stand a chance*, she thought.

Meanwhile, in the bedroom, Alexandra listened at her door, trying desperately to stay calm. Fat chance! She kept taking shallow, shuddering breaths and, worst of all, had started hiccuping.

"What's that noise?" Greg said, keeping his grip on the woman in his arms.

"I . . . don't hear anything," the small, rounded brunette stammered.

Greg shrugged, his hands trailing down her back. "You aren't angry at me, are you, Alex?"

Jill shuddered, willing the charade to be over. "No. Yes. Really, Greg, this is . . . impossible."

He brushed his lips across her hair. "Why, Alex? Deep down, haven't we both known this would happen one of these days?"

Jill struggled free, only to find Greg's hand on her wrist, leading her insistently to the couch.

"What about Cassie?" Jill gasped, falling beside Greg onto the cushions.

"I don't know how to explain it, Alex. Something happened when I saw you. Something just clicked. I think I fell in love with Cassie as . . . as a substitute for you. For some crazy reason, she reminded me of you."

"Al—Cassie reminded you of *me*?"

"Why does that surprise you?"

Sweat broke out across Jill's brow. "It doesn't. I mean . . . I don't even know what she looks like."

"Sure you do. I described her often enough in my letters."

In the bedroom Alexandra squeezed her eyes shut as the charade in the next room slowly began to fall apart.

"I mean . . . I never saw her. Descriptions can be so vague, really."

Greg smiled. "I suppose. Anyway, I really don't want to talk about Cassie. Or whoever she really was. I want to talk about us. You and me. I've always loved you, Alex. You must know that. But until today it wasn't real. Now—" he stopped, pulling her roughly against him "—it's very real, Alex. And I want to make it even more real. Tell me you want the same thing, Alex."

His hands were trailing across her shoulders. He was moving slowly, wondering just how far the woman would go before she called his bluff. He'd be the one in for a surprise if she didn't.

A precarious moment later Jill sprang from the couch. "I . . . I have to go . . . to the bathroom," she stammered, making a break instead for Alexandra's bedroom, mumbling as she ran, "It's through here. I'll . . . be . . . right out."

Once inside the room, Jill slammed the door and leaned heavily against it. She was breathing hard, her eyes filled with desperation. "Okay," she whispered, "what's your next clever idea?"

Alexandra put her fingers to Jill's lips. "Shh. He'll hear you." She hiccuped again, pulling Jill across the room. Then, still worried that Greg would overhear, she dragged her friend into her walk-in closet, shutting the door.

"Alex," Jill protested inside the dark, stuffy, confined space, "this is crazy. Give up. This is your chance to come clean. Go out there—"

"No, I can't," Alexandra pleaded, hiccuping. "Jill, you aren't being tough enough."

"Tough enough? Let me warn you, Alexandra Yates, you let this thing go any longer and I really am going to forget who I am. The man is positively irresistible."

Alexandra moaned. "I know . . . hic." Then she clasped her hand around Jill's wrist. "You've got to get rid of him. I swear, I'll never ask another favor—"

Both women gasped in unison as the closet door was flung open. Greg stood there with a diabolical sneer on his face.

"Okay, ladies, will the real Alexandra Yates please step out?"

Alexandra hiccuped.

Greg's sneer deepened as he stared coldly at her. "One shabby trick after another, Alex. Just how many more do you have up your sleeve? How many more times and ways do you think you can make a fool out of me?"

"Greg, I'm sorry... hic," Alexandra murmured miserably.

"Save it." His voice was ominously quiet. He shrugged, staring at her wan face as she stood beside Jill in the cluttered closet. "Maybe this makes us even."

And then without another word he turned and walked out of the bedroom, out of the apartment, out of her life.

"GO TALK TO HIM, Alex. He told me on the phone that he was staying at the Fairmont. I bet you can still catch him there if you hurry." Jill pulled Alexandra from the bed to her feet.

"And say what?"

Jill eyed her evenly. "Tell him that you love him, you little fool."

HE GLARED AT HER with stony contempt.

Alexandra stood in the middle of his hotel room. Greg was less than five feet away, but it might as well have been five thousand miles. He was unreachable, the chasm too wide, too deep to cross.

Her hands were trembling and her knees threatened to buckle under her.

"It's all my fault. But I've tried to explain."

Greg turned away.

She stared at the rigid set of his shoulders, the stiff, straight back. "I suppose I always knew eventually I'd get caught up in my lies. I was so desperate not to let the truth come out. And now," she said softly, "my only real regret is that I hurt the one person I truly love."

He spun around, hazel eyes burning. "You have a most peculiar way of loving, Alex. Deceit, betrayal, humiliation. If that's the way you show your love, save it for someone else. Someone who can appreciate it. Some damn fool masochist." His voice was thick with bitterness and pain and rage.

"That wasn't all I gave you." Her voice was angry. "I gave you my heart, my soul."

But she might as well have been talking to the wall. There was an echo in the silent room. Greg seemed like a stranger, the tension between them as fierce as their electric attraction once had been.

Greg turned his back again. He could feel Alexandra's pain competing with his own, but he was determined not to let that affect him. He told himself he wanted no explanations, no apologies. He told himself it was over. He tried to convince himself he wanted her to suffer, wanted to hurt her as she had hurt him.

Some perverse impulse forced Alexandra to go on despite her humiliation. "I wanted to tell you the truth so many times, Greg. I whispered a hundred unspoken apologies. You have no idea how many times I wished I'd never walked into that gallery. Never before have I wished so hard I could undo something."

He turned slowly back to face her, meeting her gaze straight-on for the first time. *No*, he thought, *even now I don't want to cause her pain.* "Some things," he said quietly, his features strained, "can't be undone."

"I suppose . . . you're right." Tears blurred her eyes, and she couldn't keep the choking sound from her voice.

She started across the room to the door. The walk seemed endless, the silence overpowering. *Say something, Greg. Call me back. Forgive me.*

Her hand turned the doorknob.

"I meant it, Alex. I never wanted anyone the way I wanted you," he said.

She froze for a moment, casting her eyes down. "I felt the same way." She opened the door. "I still do."

It wasn't until she reached the confines of the taxi that she gave vent to her pain. She cried the whole way back to her apartment, mindless of the cabdriver's uneasy concern.

Jill was waiting for her when she got back. Neither of them said a word. Jill merely gave her a sympathetic smile. Alexandra walked into her bedroom, grateful to be alone with her grief.

SHE WROTE HIM a dozen letters, mailed none of them. All of the apologies she could make had been made. All the explanations she could give had been given.

Perhaps she would have lived with her quiet misery forever if that postcard hadn't come two weeks later. It was very brief, very cool.

Dear Alex (the "Dear" was scratched out),
The Gilrand project is mine again. I thought you'd like to know.

Thanks,
Greg

"Why thank you?" Jill asked after Alexandra read it aloud.

"I'm not sure." A slow smile burgeoned on her lips as she read between the lines. "I'm not sure that's really what matters."

Jill smiled back. "You could be right."

Alexandra pressed the postcard to her heart.

"What now?" Jill asked. "It looks like Greg's put the ball in your court."

Alexandra's eyes were downright luminous. "I think I'll go with it. Return the shot. Who knows? Maybe I'll get lucky."

AS SHE STOOD outside Greg's Manhattan apartment door—she'd gotten through the building's main door thanks to an exiting tenant—Alexandra remembered how nervous she'd been the last time she'd stood here. This time everything was riding on the outcome, and yet she felt strangely calm. She rang the bell, her hand steady.

She heard his footsteps. When they stopped, he didn't open the door immediately. She could feel him looking through his peephole. And then taking another few moments to compose himself.

When he opened the door, he looked a little leaner, harder—and tired. And still the most irresistible, appealing man she'd ever set eyes on.

"Hello, Alex." His voice was flat, controlled.

"Hello, Greg."

"What are you doing here?"

"Will you ask me in?"

He hesitated and then stepped aside.

"I was happy to receive your postcard." *That's great, Alex. You win the grand prize for understatement with that one.*

She walked into the living room, Greg following her. She turned around to face him. "Why did you thank me?"

He smiled faintly. "As it turns out, my father did a lot of thinking after you attacked him that day in his garden room."

"I was angry."

There was a hint of tenderness in his eyes. "When I got back from San Francisco, he showed up at my apartment and told me New Amsterdam Life had decided to withdraw their offer on the Gilrand Estate. He even apologized. I don't think he's ever done that before in his life. The next day I got a call from the city asking if I was still interested in tackling the restoration project."

Greg crossed the room to the window. "A couple of days later I went down to Greenwich." He grinned. "Oh, by the way, the wedding never came off. Dad decided that Meg lacked depth and character."

"She didn't lack for much else," Alexandra commented wryly.

Greg laughed. "Believe me, that can wear thin very quickly."

She smiled. "I believe you."

His laughter vanished. Alexandra could see a flicker of pain in his eyes before he looked away. "My father and I had a long talk." He gave her a quick glance. She was still smiling. "We talked about a lot of things. My mother, my feelings about military boarding school, our feelings about each other. You were right all along,

Alex. He's been hurting as much as I've been hurting. And he's been just as stubborn. Just as scared. Slowly I think we're redefining the terms of our relationship. It feels . . . good." He looked directly at her then, meeting her gaze evenly. "I also talked to my father about us."

"I don't suppose he was very taken with me after our last encounter."

"You're wrong. He was very taken with you. He thought you were a breath of fresh air, the first person to be honest with him in a long time. It was me he wasn't taken with. He thinks I'm a fool. He thinks I ought to marry you."

So much for Alexandra's calm. "What did you tell him?" she asked, trembling like a leaf.

He kept his gaze steady. "I told him it was too late."

Alexandra was stunned to see that Greg's eyes were moist. "I wrote you a letter," she said in a low voice.

"I didn't receive it."

"I didn't mail it."

"What did it say?"

She started walking to him. "I'll tell you if you'll meet me halfway."

She walked a few more steps and then stopped. And waited. She felt the impulse to close her eyes, but she kept them open, kept her gaze straight on Greg.

He crossed his arms over his chest. Made no move. "That's asking for a lot, under the circumstances."

She smiled tremulously. "Under the circumstances, I'm asking for everything."

Slowly his hands dropped to his sides. More slowly still, he began to walk toward her. When he stopped only inches away from her, it took every ounce of Alexandra's willpower not to throw her arms around him.

"Okay," he said softly. "What did the letter say?"

His nearness, his familiar scent, the touch of tenderness in his voice, made it difficult for her to concentrate.

"I wrote, 'Dear Greg . . . No. My dearest Greg.'" She took a steadying breath. "'I may have lied about many things, but not about my love. I love you passionately, enduringly. This time there are no lines to read between.'" She could feel her face grow hot under Greg's steady gaze.

"Go on."

She looked away. "'I want so desperately for you to forgive me. I want a happily-ever-after ending.'" She swallowed hard. "That's what I wrote." She clutched her throat as a hiccup escaped. And then another. There was an embarrassed, almost pained expression on her face. "I . . . need . . . water," she stammered between eruptions.

She started for the kitchen, but Greg caught her shoulders.

"I have another cure."

"You do?"

He laughed. "I do, Alex. I do." Then he took her in his arms and kissed her. Alexandra responded eagerly.

Gently he drew her back. "Can I add a P.S. to that letter?"

Eyes luminous, skin flushed, breathless, she nodded.

"'I think we've put ourselves and each other through enough grief. P.P.S. It's about time we both had our happily-ever-after ending—together.'"

This time when his lips met hers, their kiss was deeper, stronger, filled with giving.

It quite took her breath away.

"My hiccups are gone. That was a terrific cure."

They both laughed, even when the hiccups came back again—much, much later that night.

Harlequin Temptation

COMING NEXT MONTH

HARLEQUIN SUPERROMANCE BRINGS YOU...

Lynda Ward

Superromance readers already know that Lynda Ward possesses a unique ability to weave words into heartfelt emotions and exciting drama.

Now, Superromance is proud to bring you Lynda's tour de force: an ambitious saga of three sisters whose lives are torn apart by the conflicts and power struggles that come with being born into a dynasty.

In *Race the Sun, Leap the Moon* and *Touch the Stars*, readers will laugh and cry with the Welles sisters as they learn to live and love on their own terms, all the while struggling for the acceptance of Burton Welles, the stern patriarch of the clan.

Race the Sun, Leap the Moon and *Touch the Stars* . . . a dramatic trilogy you won't want to miss. Coming to you in July, August and September.

The Welles Family Trilogy

The passionate saga that brought you SARAH and
ELIZABETH continues in the compelling,
unforgettable story of

Catherine

MAURA SEGER

An independent and ambitious woman earns the disapproval of Boston society when she discovers passion and
love with Irishman Evan O'Connel.